My Sister's Downfall

SM Thomas

Written by:
SM Thomas

Published by:
A.R Hurne Publishing

Edited by:
Allison Reinert, A Favorite Pen

Cover Art by:
Adrijus – Rocking Book Covers

ISBN
978-1-7385686-1-1

Dedication

Dedicated to my Mum & Dad.

Thank you for always supporting my
flights of fancy – and for reading
every one of my books (even if they
scare you a little!)

SM Thomas

CONTENTS

My Sister's Downfall

Prologue

I watch my sister float through the air like a gravity-defying ballerina, all limbs pointed as though ready for her stage debut. At the back of my mind, I can hear the anticipation of the crowd in the theatre, thrilled to witness the prima donna's debut. Their collective breath drawing in as the conductor signals the first swell of the orchestra. All eyes on her as the flashing lights outline her movement through the skyline.

I note the way her red coat dances in the wind that is growing in ferocity around her, playing with her movements as she falls. As though she's Mother Nature's favourite plaything. There are voices all around me, crying out in horror and shock as gravity pushes on.

Pulling the phone from my face, I realise that my jaw is aching. My mouth is wide, practically unhinged, as a scream fights its way from my stomach to my throat; unleashing my terror like a banshee upon the world. Even though I'm eleven stories below her I know instinctively that our cries will be synchronised in pitch. Bonded together by blood and love, creating an ominous harmony for the witnesses around us.

As expected, my legs move before I've had a chance to think through my actions. On autopilot, I am moving towards the end of her path, where an abandoned car waits unaware in a parking bay. Her cries are broken syllables now as she rushes towards the ground. I scream out her name. One singular word that I hope carries up through the air towards her. I need her to know that I'm here.

The air disappears beneath my feet as I'm hoisted from the pavement by two strong arms that wrap themselves around my waist. They prevent me from moving any closer, taking me from the biological draw towards her. I thrash around as best I can, hoping to slip from their grasp but it's no use. I can do nothing but watch as my sister lands on the roof of the car.

The noise is horrific. The collective breath now a collective cry from everyone on the street as we struggle to comprehend what we've just witnessed. She hit the car with such force that it felt like a small bomb had exploded. The sound of twisting metal giving way to a broken body harmonised poetically with the sound of shattering glass spraying over the road and into nearby lampposts. The ping ping of the shards is the only noise remaining as the car sighs in defeat and shock renders everyone silent.

Reality reels me back in and I scream her name again and again as witnesses haphazardly step towards her. I don't want her final moments to be shared with strangers. It's supposed to be me who's by her side.

The arms around my waist loosen and I break free. There's a wall of emergency service workers between me and my sister and I yell at them that I'm family, but they don't let me through. Instead, they offer me sad expressions and platitudes as they tell me she's gone, that she died on impact, that no one could have survived.

A friendly paramedic gently places his arm around my shoulder and leads me towards a waiting ambulance, concerned I'm in shock. He offers me a foil blanket as though that can solve all my problems. I take it despite doubting its effectiveness, it can't make this situation any worse. Then a familiar voice is at my side. It belongs to the person who prevented me from reaching my sister before she hit the ground - the Inspector.

"I'm so sorry for your loss," he offers. A phrase I guess I've got to get used to all over again now. Another funeral for me to sit through and bite my tongue. As though praying will bring her peace just as it did our parents. The dead can't feel peace. The dead can't feel anything.

Loss is the wrong word though. I didn't lose anything, that implies being careless. And I'm never careless.

All I can do is nod my head at him. I don't think I could find the words right now. The paramedic is right, I am suffering from shock. As a chill creeps up my spine I pull the foil blanket closer around myself, grateful now for its presence.

My sister is dead.

My sister has died.

And it is all my fault.

Chapter One: Isabella

"This is unacceptable, you must see that." Andrew, my campaign manager is incredulous, which he's making obvious in the way he's speaking to the poor Inspector in front of us. Andrew isn't a man to mince his words, especially where I'm concerned.

I watch the Inspector's face, hoping for a twitch of his lip that shows his annoyance but none comes. Either this man is the world's best poker player or he's been working this job long enough that unfounded rage aimed in his direction is water off a duck's back.

"I understand your concerns, Mr. Carter," the Inspector places his left hand on the surface of my desk as he talks, and I note the lack of a wedding ring.

There's no denying that the Inspector is a very attractive man. He's older than me, just my type, and his salt and peppered hair only serves to highlight his strong jawbone and dark eyes.

"Blackmail is something we take very seriously in the force, especially when it comes to members of political parties." He turns his attention to me now and offers me a comforting smile. It stirs animalistic butterflies in my stomach. I really need to get out more.

"I promise you, we will get to the bottom of this, Mrs. Thompson."

"Miss," I correct him, unable to help the flirtatious smile that comes with it. "And I know you will, Inspector Coulson."

"Please, call me James." He keeps his mouth in a straight line but I notice the twinkle in his eye. Perhaps he's feeling the same chemistry I am or maybe he's wondering why I appear so laid back considering the note left for me this morning.

Five words, written in red paint to give the illusion of blood.

I know what you did.

I admit when I first found the note on my desk inside my locked and alarmed office it did cause me some concern. Right after calling Andrew, my prone-to-dramatics campaign manager, I logged a call to security, asking them for an access report for my office.

The report showed that my office had been accessed using my security pass at 2 a.m. How convenient that this was the time the CCTV tapes were switched over for the day. Whoever left that note had inside knowledge - which meant it was an issue we could have dealt with internally.

But no, Andrew had to get the police involved. The gossip would be all over the tabloids by this evening; clearly what the perpetrator was after. We were giving them the attention they craved, which would only encourage them. I've learnt it's always best to starve the trolls rather than feed into their games.

I was the youngest female member of Parliament to hold my seat, and now, after three years of constant graft, I was in line to become the youngest and first female head of our party. I wasn't sure if it was because of my age or my gender that the press had such an interest in me, but this wouldn't help matters.

They'd paint me as a damsel in distress, make out that politics were too dangerous a game for me, and the voters might buy into that narrative, something I couldn't afford.

If I didn't have the public onside then I sure as hell didn't have the faith of my party onside. They needed a leader who could win the next election, and a lost little girl wasn't that leader.

Andrew may have fanned those flames with his call to the police, but I suppose I can't be too harsh on him. We had some news last week that rattled us both - an ex-boyfriend of mine was found murdered and left with a red hankie covering his face. The deep royal red of my parties flagship colour.

I'd recently heard through the grapevine that he was planning a kiss-and-tell with one of the more tawdry tabloids but I hadn't let it bother me. I was confident that my track record would survive any saucy secrets he might share. Andrew had wanted to buy him off but I'd refused.

If word got out it would just open the floodgates for more vermin to come sniffing around for their piece of flesh. Nothing came of the fodder, although we had prepared for it. I penned several personal press releases expressing my disappointment in my ex and in the journalists who associated themselves with these kinds of assassination attempts and the distribution of revenge porn.

But we never had to use them. No article ever appeared. And then news of his death trickled through my social grapevine until it landed on my phone in the form of a text message from a long-forgotten mutual acquaintance. She thought I deserved to know the news of his death first-hand, and I was grateful for her consideration.

He might have been an ex from a long time ago, but he had been a part of my life for a good two years before we split. It gave me ten minutes to centre myself before the press put two and two together and Andrew was called to get my statement on the matter.

So yes, I completely understood why the note had led to Andrew calling the local station and demanding their best Inspector take on the case personally. I don't know why he kept referring to it as blackmail though, no demands for money had been left on the note. Just those five words.

I know what you did.

Those five words that I knew couldn't be true. Which is why all the worry in my body evaporated as I changed my security code. That was the end of that I told myself.

"Thank you for your time today James." I like the feel of his name on my tongue and I can tell from the shift in his posture that he does too. "We'll let you know if we receive any more messages but I imagine the situation has now resolved itself with the change of my security code. Probably just a disgruntled employee trying to unnerve me."

"They're probably getting a pay cheque from the opposition," adds Andrew with a snarling tone and I glare at him.

"That's a very serious accusation, Mr. Carter," says James and he's not wrong. Underhanded techniques like that are taken very seriously these days in Parliament. And it's not an accusation we can afford to make without strong evidence.

"Forgive my campaign manager. He spoke out of turn out of emotion because he was concerned for my well-being." For a moment it looks as though Andrew is going to protest my claim, but he must catch the gleam in my eyes as he has the good sense to keep his mouth shut.

"Of course, completely understandable. Please do keep me up to date on any developments, or if you think of any useful information. I'll be happy to come back out anytime." Now I'm certain the Inspector is flirting with me, there's no reason for his eyes to linger on my lips as he talks. Not the brightest idea I've ever had, to develop a crush on a cop, but that's the way the cookie crumbles.

"Thank you again for your time." I stand and extend a hand, he follows suit and his handshake lasts a little longer than is necessary. Then Andrew shows him out of my office and I find myself feeling a little put out that I'll have no need to see Inspector Coulson again. Of that I'm certain. This has just been a dark prank, the result of somebody becoming far too bored on a night shift.

I suppose there's a sense of relief to be had in the fact Andrew called the police over my sister. If I thought his reaction was dramatic, then hers would have blown it out of the water.

My older sister has always looked out for me. I was fifteen when our parents passed away. I was already fully raised, as far as I was concerned and ready to unleash myself on the world, but May insisted we stay together as a family. Despite only being eighteen herself, she did her best to give me all that I needed and then some. My constant protector and champion.

All I had to do now was grow a backbone and call her. She'd never forgive me if she learnt about the note through the press rather than from the horse's mouth. I don't know how she's managed to cope since I won my seat and had to sign the Official Secrets Act - she'd grown so used to knowing about every moment of my day that it must drive her mad knowing there are parts of me she's no longer privy to. I mean, I kept secrets from her long before my career in politics, but now she knows there are things I don't tell her.

I take a deep breath and pick my mobile phone up from the desk where I left it. Holding it towards my face

I wait until it has scanned my features and then offer it my thumbprint.

All Government-issued phones now have two levels of biometric security enabled, since a few too many of my colleagues had a habit of leaving their phones or briefcases on public transportation and now the ship is run so tightly it's impossible for it to leak. That's the theory anyway.

Leaks still happen. That's the problem with relying on humans. Humans are fallible. And prone to accepting bribes or acting rashly out of jealousy. We've already rooted out two rats in my office alone, Lord knows how many there are working within the walls of the Houses of Common.

Christ - that's probably who's responsible for the note - the goddamn rats we fired. Despite firm evidence that they were both guilty of speaking to the press, they pleaded their innocence to my face as security escorted them to pack up their desks. Andrew had told me I didn't need to come in and witness their dismissal, but I wanted to look into the whites of their eyes and have them know the level of my disappointment. I must tell Andrew of my suspicions when he returns. He'll know what to do.

I scroll through my recent call history until I find my last call with May. It had only been last night but already it was thirty lines down on the list. We'd spent twenty minutes on the phone together as we each cooked our dinners, a daily ritual that meant we had at least one verbal touch point every twenty-four hours.

By now, she was more of a friend than a sister, something thirteen-year-old me never would have believed. We used to fight like cats and dogs, like most siblings, but now we just want the best for one another and we make sure to celebrate every little win the other achieves in life. That's the problem with it being just the two of us, we have to be the entire cheering squad for every occasion.

My sister is a very well-liked accountant in a central London firm. She could easily move positions. She's constantly headhunted, and has been offered the role of Financial Director at other companies - but she's happy where she is. She's been with the company for thirteen years and has turned her role into a hybrid one. This gave her the perfect excuse to start thinking about getting a pet.

It's been a year since she started the search and sometimes I wonder if she prefers window shopping for an animal over the responsibility of owning one. Can't say I blame her. I'm not a fan of keeping things alive either - it's too much responsibility having to know where they are at all times, making sure they behave themselves. It's exhausting just to think about it. I guess I'm lacking any maternal instincts.

The dial tone rings at least three times, as it always does before her voice comes over the line. Sometimes I imagine her sitting at her desk, hand poised over the phone, waiting for those three bars of music to play before answering. She's a creature of habit for sure, but she's my creature of habit and that's a comfort. I cross my fingers as she greets me, hoping she'll take the news about the note exactly how she ought to. Just an interesting tidbit about my day.

Chapter Two - May

"What do you mean it was in your office?" I know my tone is sharp, and I hate speaking to her like this but she doesn't sound like she's taking this threatening note seriously.

Just as I knew she wouldn't.

That's right.

I sent my sister the note.

Go ahead and judge me all you like but it's my job as her older sister - her only family - to make sure Isabella keeps her wits about her.

I'd hoped that my note would have woken her up a little to the dangers her career choice brings alongside it, but she isn't rattled, not even in the slightest. We live in a day and age where MP's are consistently threatened every time they speak out on any matter. In someone's eyes they are always wrong.

Social media is full of keyboard warriors, and all it takes is one individual to take things to an extreme and a tragedy happens. I didn't want Isabella to become a statistic so I had no choice but to take matters into my own hands. I had to give her a controlled scare so she realises she needs to be more cautious. She still hosts open meetings with members of the public without a full team of security for Christ's sake.

I can tell from the words she's choosing as she explains the situation to me, that she simply isn't worried about the threat or what it could lead to. Or maybe it's because she knows that she doesn't have any secrets someone could spill. My little sister has always been honest to a fault. It's why the voters like her so much, it's why she'll win the leadership contest, and it's why she'll end up being Prime Minister one day.

And I want all of that for her. I genuinely, hand-on-heart do. There's nothing I want more in life than to see Isabella achieve her dreams. I just want her to learn to be a little more careful in her pursuit of them. One day she could have a real lunatic on her tail and she won't be able to simply brush it aside as the actions of a disgruntled employee.

I've been sat at my desk all day waiting for her to call, expecting her worried breathy tones down the line from the moment the clock ticked to 9 a.m. But her call never came in the morning. At first, I told myself she was too shocked to reach out to me but as I picked apart my ham and pickle sandwich at lunchtime I realised that I wasn't her first port of call anymore. She had other people to fill that role. More specifically she had Andrew to fill that role.

Andrew, the man who has managed her campaigns since she first won the student union elections in her final year at university. He's been by her side ever since. An irritating tumour that grows in power every year that passes. Once upon a time, she would have asked me to proofread her press releases, but now it was Andrew's sign-off that mattered. Andrew's approval that held weight.

I'd never gotten on with the man and wasn't intending to start anytime soon. The memory of the date she set us up on still makes me laugh. She truly believed we'd been a match made in heaven, when the only thing we had in common was our fixation with her. We both wanted what was best for her, to support her on the path to party leadership but there was something about Andrew that just didn't sit right with me.

Maybe it was the uneven, oblong shape of his eyebrows, or maybe it was the information I'd managed to find on the Internet about him - a few unfavourable reviews from previous clients of his that I briefly investigated.

They all ended up leading to a dead end, literally in one case, and I eventually ran out of threads to follow. For one reason or another though, I trusted the man about as much as I trusted the net zero policies of global corporations. I truly didn't want to remove the man from Isabella's life, she relied on him heavily and he did good work. But if he wasn't the man he said he was, then I would have no choice. One day the skeletons will spill from his closet, I'm sure of it.

It stung knowing that he was the person she obviously called when she found the note. But by the time I was sipping on my 3 p.m. coffee, I'd gotten over it - after all she was a professional and calling her campaign manager had been the logical thing to do. I knew that eventually I would receive her call, and that when I did it meant she finally felt vulnerable enough to reach out to me. That she truly needed me.

It would mean I wasn't just a cog in the political machine designed to protect her reputation. Yes, I was more important than Andrew, I was someone she truly cared about, which meant I would be her last call of the day. The one to settle her nerves so she could go home and sleep peacefully.

Remembering this I soften my tone, she is my younger sister after all. It's my job to support her.

"I'm sorry I raised my voice," I apologise, cradling the phone between my neck and my shoulder. "I'm just shocked."

"That's okay, I know you're just worried. It unnerved me as well."

"Do you want me to come out and meet you? I could cook us dinner?" I ask, subconsciously crossing my fingers that she'll say yes. We haven't had a home-cooked meal together in so long. We might talk every night but we only manage to meet up in person once a week. And it's usually a snatched sandwich in some back lane pub where my sister won't be spotted by any of the locals. Hardly the place for sisterly bonding.

"No, I'm okay. I think Andrew has organised a car to take me home tonight - save me getting a taxi. And I've got a ton of emails to catch up on. Today really played havoc with my schedule."

I give the impression of listening and sympathising but inside I'm beginning to seethe. Of course Andrew is taking care of everything. He always does. Doesn't he know that's my role in life? That it's been that way since our parents died? It's always been me and Isabella, with the occasional guest spot for other halves when we have them.

Even when we'd both had partners we still centred our lives around each other, still called the other first with good news or bad. Well, it had been that way for most of the time anyway.

There had been Chris who'd managed to upgrade himself to a series regular in our lives the day he put a ring on my finger - but obviously that hadn't lasted. Even he couldn't put up with the bond between me and my sister. He always felt side-lined and in one heated argument, I told him that he always would be. That had been the week before he left without so much as a note.

I called him repeatedly but his phone had gone straight to voicemail each time, until eventually it didn't even connect. He must have changed his name on social media because I've not been able to find a trace of him since that day. If only I'd had the chance to meet his parents when we were together, but the three of them were estranged and I never had the opportunity to mend the wounds between them.

Sometimes, when I've had a few too many glasses of wine, I get stuck in a dream I can't quite place when I wake up. A broken conversation between two voices, growing more and more heated with each passing moment. Until the argument is interrupted by Isabella as she holds me in her arms and Chris fades away to nothing.

I'm sure there's some subconscious meaning behind that dream but I don't want to risk looking too deeply into it. Something tells me I'll uncover a memory best left forgotten. It's why I try not to think too hard about why my hand chose those five words to write on the note I left her.

I know what you did.

My sister is an open book, always has been, so why did my brain think that was the right turn of phrase to get a reaction from her? She's never done anything she's ashamed of, that much I'm sure of. "Life is for living" she used to tell me as we blossomed into young women. This was a way to entice me to join her for a night out, and she didn't care about how many eyes were upon her as she danced to the Macarena on a nearly empty dance floor. No, my sister has never done anything she's ashamed of, nothing she'd want to keep hidden.

After I lost Chris, Isabella had been beside herself when I stumbled bleary-eyed into her flat. I tried to hold myself together, I really had. But after two days of living alone in the flat we once shared, I had reached my mental breaking point. I spent the hour-and-a-half train journey between our locations openly bawling as I stared at the landscapes shooting past. The ticket Inspector had been kind when he noticed the engagement ring on my hand.

Cups of tea were sent my way with his compliments and when we finally reached my stop he held my hand as I stepped down onto the platform. He was obviously a father and had seen that kind of heartache before. I stayed with my sister for three days after my shock arrival. She dropped everything to be with me.

It's one of the few times in our lives I've let her take care of me. Eventually though, after another short stay in the Sanctuary, I pulled myself together and used the open return option on my ticket - after all the tax returns at work weren't going to file themselves.

"May, are you still there?" she asks and I take a breath. I'd let myself get lost down memory lane and had forgotten she was speaking to me.

"Sorry, sorry, yes I'm still here."

"You sound busy, I should go."

"No, no. I'm never too busy for you. Did you want to call me from the car just in case you're nervous?"

"Why would I be nervous? I mean, yes the fact somebody has been in my office was a little shocking, but the note itself was innocuous. I'm sure once I get home, I'll feel completely like myself again."

She was giving herself a pep talk and using me as a sounding board. It's what she always did when the world seemed a little out of her control. I didn't mind, at least it means I still have my uses.

This would be the perfect chance to tell her that actually I'm currently in her hometown. That I've rented a hot desk in an office opposite hers. That I'm staying in a small hotel just down the road from her house. That I can be with her within twenty minutes. But I don't tell her any of that and I don't know why.

Maybe it's because she hasn't asked me to help her. Maybe it's because I'm nervous about her rejection should I offer it. Whatever the reason, I find myself keeping a secret from my sister for the second time in twenty-four hours. I don't like the feeling.

"Of course, absolutely. You get yourself home, maybe have a bubble bath and unwind. I'm sure you're right and this is nothing to worry about," I say.

"Exactly. Like I said to Andrew, it's probably just one of the pencil pushers we let go last week for speaking to the press."

I wince at the term pencil pushers. My sister might mean no harm by it but she's always made it clear that there are some careers she values above others. And office workers such as myself are on a lower rung to others. Such as her.

"Absolutely. Absolutely." I'm repeating my words, something I used to do when I found myself lost for the right ones.

Please Isabella, please just tell me you need me. My life is so empty without Chris. It has been for years. I've sat here festering whilst watching her shine. All I want is to support her, to feel needed by her, to have a purpose in her life.

"Right, well I'll speak to you later?" she asks.

"Of course. 7 p.m.?"

"What are you cooking tonight?"

I move to the carrier bag by my legs and pick up a pack of instant noodles and turn them over in my hand.

"Oh, I was thinking maybe a lasagne, that way I can freeze the leftovers for lunch," I lie, making a mental note to make an online order tonight at my local supermarket. I'm going to go home in the morning and get my shit together. I need to get my life back in order. For too long I've tied my mental well-being to my little sister when it's clear she no longer needs me. Starting tomorrow it's a new me.

"You're so organised! I'll probably just have some kind of omelette." She laughs gently at me, believing me to be the same Type-A sister she's always known.

If only she knew the truth about what was happening to me, about the impending mental breakdown and burnout that's causing me to act so out of character. If she knew I was the one who'd left the note then she wouldn't hesitate to send me back to the Sanctuary.

I shudder at the memory. True it had been the very best mental healthcare money could buy. Isabella had spared no expense, but still, to this day, I'm not sure my second three-month stay with them had been warranted.

Yes, I had been broken when Chris left me.

Yes, there are still sizable gaps in my memory from that time.

But hand-on-heart I don't believe I'd required those endless hours of psychiatric care and medication, no matter what outlandish claims I'd been vocalising.

I can't let it get that far again. I can't start making unfounded accusations and wind up back in care. From now on there will be no more notes. No more games. I'm just going to get back to my life and back to being regular old May.

"I'll speak to you in a few hours," I say, desperately trying to end the call. Tears are choking my throat that I won't be able to explain away to her. Tears that she'll want answers for.

It happens more often than not these days. Sometimes it feels like my eyes have a mind of their own as I'll be merrily typing away on my laptop and find that my face is damp. Nothing sad will have entered my mind and yet my tears are flowing.
 Thankfully the company I work for allows me to work remotely as it's a rather embarrassing infliction.

"Okay, love you," she says.

"I love you too."

I hang up as quickly as I can and send a thanks to the heavens that I'm the only one currently in this unfamiliar open-plan office. I don't have to explain myself to anyone as I let the tears fall.

Chapter Three - Isabella

I'm sitting in the hairdresser's chair when the first text comes through. A number I don't recognise with a message I'm now familiar with.

I know what you did.

My shoulders must have tensed because my stylist Lynsey noticed.

"You okay Bella?" She asks.

I don't let many people call me Bella. It's not necessarily a name I'm comfortable with. It doesn't hold as much authority as Isabella, it doesn't feel as serious and I've always been desperate to be taken seriously. May finally stopped calling me it last year but it took a lot of convincing and a lot of unanswered texts until she finally listened.

I trained her in the way one might train a dog - I ignored her whenever she called me Bella. Eventually, she realised the only way to get a response was to use the name I preferred. It did feel a little mean at the time but in the end, it achieved the desired result.

"Yeah, sorry - I've just got to take care of this," I reply, not wanting to worry her.

Lynsey is different though. She's been doing my hair since I was eleven. She used to do my mum's hair and it was from my mum she learnt to shorten my name. Plus she isn't in my life every day like my sister so it's more of a sporadic pull on my heartstrings when I hear it rather than a daily one.

My relationship with my mother, well my parents, is more complicated than I care to delve into, but I think in some ways most children miss their parents when they're gone. Ever since they passed though, my life has been on an upward trajectory so I can't say it disrupted things too much.

May, on the other hand. Oh, poor May was completely broken by their deaths. Full of guilt and regrets. It was the first time she experienced memory blackouts, which led to all kinds of paranoid thought trains she was unable to depart from.

I was the one who pushed her to see a doctor at the time, her words were becoming too spiteful to bear and sooner or later would lead to gossip I couldn't come back from. And I knew that she would never want that for me. Not really. My sister has always wanted me to succeed.

My first instinct on receiving the text is to screenshot it and send it to Andrew. Let him deal with it. Then I remember Inspector Coulson. Perhaps this is an update I should pass on personally. Luckily I saved James' contact details already so it was simply a case of composing a text of the right tone and forwarding him the screenshot.

Hi James,
You said to get in touch if I received any more notes, as you can see, whoever it is has moved to texts now. Perhaps we should meet up so you can view it in person?
Isabella

Perfect. There was no suggestion of worry in my words, and therefore, nothing that could be misconstrued as me being a damsel in distress, an idea I loathe. I have never been in distress and I don't intend to start now. I don't want him, or anyone, to see me as a victim.

I can still feel the sting of people's sympathy at my parents' funeral - their empty apologies and worried glances across the church as May and I sat strong in the front pew. I don't need anyone to feel sorry for me. Not when my parents died and not now. There was nothing in life that I couldn't handle. I'd proved that time and time again.

My phone pings back almost instantly.

Isabella,
I would definitely appreciate the chance to view the message in person. Shall I come to your office around 5? In the meantime please block the number.
James

I smile to myself as I think of all the times in my life when an evening meeting rolled into an early dinner - I hope tonight is no different. If I can just keep the Inspector occupied for an hour then it would be polite to invite him to join me for dinner, not presumptuous. I would just be behaving like a considerate person. Maybe I'd take him to the Italian restaurant just round the corner from my office. It was cosy, with chairs placed close together. I could accidentally brush against him all night.

The idea of doing so gives me a chill up my spine. Plus the owner usually gave me a table in the back away from prying eyes. Discretion was built into the service fee, but I didn't mind. It was a small price to pay when you conducted the kind of business I usually did.

"Who's making you smile?" Lynsey asks me as she begins the long and arduous process of adding what feels like three hundred bleach foils to my hair.

"A new friend," I reply, catching her eye in the mirror as she gives me a mischievous wink.

Four hours later and I'm in my office, waiting for the front desk to let me know that James has arrived. I nipped home after my trip to the hairdresser's to put on one of my favourite outfits. It's nothing particularly special or spectacular - a simple black dress as far as anyone else would know. But it always makes me feel like I could take on the world and I fancied a bit of a confidence boost right now.

I inadvertently let Andrew know about the text message and the fact that I informed the Inspector.

He has unrestricted access to my personal calendar and, therefore, gets a notification whenever I block out any time, which I had done immediately after James confirmed he would visit.

It's not that Andrew is controlling. It means I'm able to take care of any personal matters and he organises my work commitments around them without me having to tell him about my every move. It's a time saver honestly, but an annoying one today.

He had tried to insist that he needed to be present for this meeting. He had to hear first-hand what James' plan of action was regarding the messages.

Unfortunately for Andrew, something more important came up that required his attention and he could no longer be in my office at the allotted time. So when the call came from Reception and the Inspector was on his way to see me, I was thankfully alone. Exactly as I wanted.

I open my office door at the same moment he'd been about to knock and we share an embarrassed laugh at the situation. It breaks the ice. I'm not often nervous around people but something about James gives me butterflies in my stomach. There's a sense of danger in indulging this flirtation. It's probably why Andrew wanted to be here tonight - to cock-block me from making any stupid decisions.

My whole life people have thought they knew what was best for me, and my whole life those people have let me down with their own poor decision making. Andrew was no different from my parents or my sister. Thought he knew better than I did.

Yes, inviting James here with seduction in mind was a rash decision, but it was my decision to make. The problem with people is they don't see their own flaws.

Andrew, for example, thinks his controlling nature is a positive when really it robs him of experiencing life to its fullest. If you never see where life takes you, then you'll never know your journey to its natural completion. Andrew is just as flawed as I am, but at least I know my own faults.

"I understand one of your exes has recently passed away?" He says it as though it's a question but we both know he's simply stating facts.

"Well, if there was ever the perfect conversation opener…," I reply with a light laugh and gesture towards the sofa at the back of my office for us to sit. I slip off my heels and tuck my feet underneath myself, turning my body towards him.

"Sorry, I have a habit of speaking before I think. What I mean is this increases our interest in the notes and messages," he replies and I'm mildly disappointed that his mind is solely on the case.

"I'm sure they aren't related. I haven't thought about Marcus in years, there's barely a link between us anymore."

"But he was found with a hankie over his face, in your parties colours," he says and I fight back a sigh. Of course, I know this. It was the point that May kept bringing up after it had happened. I saw the crime scene photos first-hand thanks to a friend in a different department to James.

I could describe the hankie to you with my eyes closed. It was so ingrained in my memory. But now wasn't the time to speak about a hankie.

"Red is a very common colour, Inspector, and back when I knew Marcus he liked to think of himself as a gentleman. It wouldn't surprise me to learn that the hankie was his."

"You shouldn't dismiss the link so quickly." He's trying to get me to take this seriously, and I do take it seriously. I really do. I'm just not prepared to let any of it rattle me enough to show it. Whoever is behind these messages wants a reaction and I will not debase myself to give them one.

"I'm not dismissing it, James," I see the twitch of a smile at the edge of his eyes as I speak his name, "I'm simply trying to keep the bigger picture in focus. The chances are much more likely that the two incidents are not linked. Marcus, God rest his soul, had a habit of upsetting the wrong types of people and the notes are most likely the work of a disgruntled ex-employee."

"A while ago he was trying to sell a story about you, that must have at least put him back onto your radar," he counters.

"Yes, of course it did. But nothing ever came of it. I don't even know what information he was trying to sell. Probably old personal photographs knowing him." I run my hand through my hair, hoping to draw his attention towards my face and away from this case. Marcus' death has nothing to do with the notes. I'm sure of it.

"Well, between you and me, there's a special place in hell reserved for people who do that." His shoulders swell as he speaks and I know that revenge porn and the people behind it clearly touches a nerve. It's sweet and causes the butterflies at his presence to swell.

"Thank you." I lay a hand on his arm and gently squeeze it. "It's nice to meet someone who understands how awful it can feel." Tears are beginning to prickle at the side of my eyes and he notices.

"Anyway, let's not waste any more time talking about him. If you're certain you feel confident the two are unrelated, then I'm happy to go along with that - unless we hear otherwise."

I nod and we hold eye contact for a beat longer than is needed. He has to be feeling the tension too. I haven't moved my hand from his arm yet. The heat in my palm is growing the longer I leave it there.

"Did you find anything out about the texts?" I ask, noticing that time isn't moving quite as fast as I want it to. It's still too early for me to invite him for dinner. It would be too obvious to do it now.

"Dead end I'm afraid. They came from a burner phone that was purchased this morning from a corner shop without CCTV. The owner had an agency cashier working that particular shift and the kid barely looked up from his tablet when he served them."

"Male or female?" As much as I'm sure the notes and messages are a disgruntled employee I'd still like to know for definite. You should always know your enemies as well as you know yourself. It's the only way to stay safe. Plus, if we could identify them before James did, then we could deal with the problem internally without any pesky leaks to the press.

"Kid said he doesn't remember. Not sure if I believe him, but there's only so hard I can press without having an official reason. No threats have been made nor money demanded as of this moment; this is just an irritation as far as my boss is concerned."

"Does that mean you're dropping the case?" God, I hope not. I know he should. I know this is a waste of police resources as well as my precious time but I need an excuse to keep seeing him. At least for now.

"Not at all. What I do in my own time is my own business and I've got a feeling about these messages. I don't think it's as simple as a nuisance caller."

He glances at his watch and disappointment washes over me as I realise he must have somewhere better to be. Probably a girlfriend waiting at home for him, after all, a lack of a wedding ring didn't necessarily symbolise availability.

"It's starting to get on a bit," he says. "Shall we continue this conversation over dinner?"

I'm too shocked to reply instantly. I thought I'd been the one with the master plan, the one who was in control of this situation, but it turns out Inspector James Coulson had his mind elsewhere too.

"There's a lovely Italian round the corner if you fancy it?" I offer in response and he smiles and nods. It doesn't matter how a victory is won. Only that it is.

Chapter Four - May

She went out with that man last night.

Nearly went home with him too.

What does she really know about this Inspector?

He was awfully keen to take on her case, and practically bolted up the stairs to her office after she received the first note. I watched him arrive. Has she, even once, asked herself why he's so interested in her?

Of course she hasn't. Isabella lives in the moment without a worry for the consequences. She does what she needs to do, and what she wants to do, and lets the pieces fall into place around her.

I picked up another burner phone last night. In fact, I picked up several. The lad from the corner shop where I bought the first one had been really helpful in stocking me up, and he'd promised to forget any detail of me - for the right price of course. I was more than happy to pay though. Isabella is my sister and I can't put a price on her safety. Plus, I respect his entrepreneurial spirit.

Last night, after our phone call, I'd been ready to pack up my meagre belongings, return home and leave this madness behind me. Surely Isabella was more safety conscious than I gave her credit, she probably had countless protocols in place to protect her that I didn't know about. She wasn't flippant with her life, I told myself.

But then I'd seen her walking out of her office building with that stranger and into a restaurant, and I knew I couldn't abandon her. Not until she started being more cautious. Andrew isn't much of a manager, either, as he was nowhere to be seen - surely now, with this threat hanging over her head he should be glued to her side.

I seethed about it the whole bus ride back to my hotel. My mood wasn't helped by the 'inspirational' art prints that adorned my room's walls, nor did the squeaking kettle help calm my nerves as I waited for it to boil.

I turned on the television in my room for some background noise, a way to keep my brain busy and tried to focus on anything else, but it was no use. All I could think about as I lay on the lacklustre mattress was Isabella and the Inspector.

So I've come up with a new plan. I'm going to tackle this issue head-on. I'm sure she isn't going to appreciate my interference but once I know she's safe, I can go back home, back to my own life, and get myself together. It will be so much easier for me to do that if my mind isn't constantly on high alert worrying about her.

This morning I decided to bypass the office block that holds my rented hot desk, and instead head for the tall glimmering building that houses my sister's offices. Between she and her staff, they take up the entire tenth floor and I couldn't be more proud of all she's achieved.

It's been a long time since I've visited her here. I think the last time I stepped foot through these doors was when I was invited to the opening party two years ago when she first signed the lease. My sister prefers to keep her family and her work as separate as physically possible. Can't say I blame her given my recent behaviour.

The receptionist at the front desk doesn't notice our family resemblance and gestures towards a nearby armchair for me to wait in whilst he finishes his call. It's a personal call as far as I can tell; far too much laughter for it to be a professional one. No one enjoys their job that much.

I have to admit I'm a little taken aback. Throughout our youth, we were told how alike we looked. Mum used to joke that she'd cloned a miniature version of me. For this man not to notice the symmetry of our features is a testament to how we're both ageing.

Granted, part of Isabella's job is to always look presentable. I know she gets her hair done every three weeks, and despite her denial, I'm certain there's a touch or two of Botox in her forehead - but I didn't think we looked that drastically different these days.

Sure my level of skincare extended to picking up whatever moisturiser was on offer when I did my weekly shop, and yes my hair colour comes from a box, but I just can't believe that's enough to have robbed me of my resemblance to my sister.

"I'm so sorry, how can I help you?" the receptionist asks after finally hanging up on the caller. At least he has the customer service skill set in place to sound genuine in his apology.

"Hi, I'm here to see Isabella," I begin and I notice his eyes flick over to the security guard by the door.

Everyone in the building is on high alert where Isabella is concerned. The guard's presence is a comfort. At least someone is taking the perceived threat against my sister seriously.
"I'm her sister, May."

His face goes slack as he takes in our family nose and jawline and I can tell he's kicking himself for not noticing it sooner. A warm feeling of vindication strokes my cheeks - I knew I didn't look that much different from Isabella despite the helping hands she may have had.

"She isn't expecting me, sorry. I should have called ahead." The concern he briefly showed for her safety when he eyed up security has thawed my resentment towards him for continuing his call. I don't want him to think he's missed a meeting update in her calendar or to worry that he'll be reprimanded in any way.

"I wanted to surprise her. Foolish really, I know how busy she is."

He smiles at me warmly now and steps out from behind his desk.

"How about I pop you into one of the conference rooms whilst I let her know that you're here? That way you can relax and have a warm drink whilst you wait."

He guides me towards a side office and I'm pleasantly surprised to see one of those fancy pod coffee machines waiting for me. I'd always wanted to try one but couldn't justify the expense for just me in my home office.

"That's very kind of you. I appreciate it. Please tell her not to hurry, I'm sure I'll be quite comfortable in here." He flashes me another warm smile before departing and I know I've done my job.

I've charmed him, made him think that I'm better than I am. He's bought into the vision I always try to portray of myself, the one that Chris had loved so dearly. But Chris must have eventually seen the cracks appear in my facade.

Why else would he leave without saying goodbye? He'd proposed to me using his family ring, and he hadn't even got in touch to ask for it back. It was something that still bothered me all these years later. I never met his parents as they were estranged, so I had no way of contacting them to discuss the matter myself.

The receptionist has only been gone for three minutes when my phone vibrates. My actual phone that is, not the burner tucked inside one of the internal pockets of my bag.

A message from Isabella.

This is amazing! I can't believe you're actually here. I'll be down as soon as I can.

Warmth spreads through my stomach as I re-read her message. My sister loves me. She really does. I shouldn't be doing any of this to her. She's a grown woman who can take care of herself. I'm her sister, not her mother. She doesn't need me to teach her life lessons anymore. I need to stop. It's hard though when it's been just the two of us for so long.

Can't wait. Couldn't resist surprising you!

I reply and then slip my phone back into my handbag.

Right, time for a coffee. I stand and move towards the machine. Just as I'm trying to figure out what syrup I want added to my drink, there's a knock at the door - Isabella was quicker than I expected.

To my complete disappointment though, it's Andrew who stands behind the door. Andrew with his stupid symmetrical face and dusty blonde hair. Andrew with that know-it-all smirk and his obnoxious mouth breathing. Andrew who pulls all my sister's strings these days.

"Oh. Hello Andrew." I move back towards the coffee machine, putting as much distance between the two of us as possible. I have no interest in spending time with this man.

"May." He greets me simply by name, not wasting any breath on pleasantries. I should be grateful that he's sparing me from partaking in dreaded small talk.

In another life maybe I could have been friends with Andrew. He does have most of the qualities I appreciate in a person. He's loyal, tenacious, and organised; the qualities that I strive for in my personality. I can see why Isabella set us up on a date. On paper we should be perfect for each other.

But what's perfect on paper only translates to reality with the right level of care and time - neither of which I was willing to give to Andrew. He was my usurper and like Catherine of Aragon, I wasn't about to go quietly. I was determined to make the transition as difficult as possible for him.

I'd call the office, make a booking to see my sister via him and then not arrive. When Isabella asked me what had happened, I'd deny ever making the appointment. Anything I could do to make him look incapable of supporting her then I did it. I signed her up to mailing lists using his details, and took to updating her Wikipedia page in the dead of night in the hopes he wouldn't notice until after she did - you name it, I did it.

I was the queen of sabotage in the first two months of his official career as my sister's full-time campaign manager. Before that point in time, he'd simply been an annoying insect in my life, constantly buzzing on the peripheral. A thorn in my side left over from her days at university. That all changed when he dropped his remaining clients to focus solely on her career. And then Chris had come along and pulled my focus.

Sweet, wonderful and funny Chris. It's been nearly three years since he left my life and I still turn to check his reaction when something dramatic happens in a movie. He was one of those people that easily got lost in imaginary worlds. It was as entertaining watching him as it was watching the show itself.

We met at work. Such a cliche. Something I swore I'd never do. Dad always taught us not to shit where we eat. When I met Chris though, all my father's teachings went out the window. We clicked instantly - one of those meet-cutes I used to roll my eyes at in movies. Walking nearly face-first into each other around a corner. He'd stepped back first and greeted me with a smile.

"One hell of an introduction," he'd said chuckling and I couldn't help but return his good nature. We walked back to our desks together, lost in mindless chatter. We found many reasons that day to go over to the other, with questions or advice that didn't need to be asked or shared. By the end of the week, we'd moved to sharing a table in the canteen every lunch break, and within a month we'd gone on our first official date.

Isabella had been taken with the idea of Chris at first. She was excited to meet him, happy I found somebody who loved me as much as she did. However, her feelings seemed to cool when the two of them finally met. Almost as though somebody had been whispering in her ear, planting seeds of doubt about him.

In hindsight I'm sure it was Andrew. He always wanted to drive a wedge between us sisters, and her disapproval of my big romance certainly achieved that. The more she warned me about moving too fast, the quicker I wanted to move.

She barely even mustered a joyful tone when I called her to tell her about the engagement. That one had stung. I guess I understood some of her worries at the time, assuming it all stemmed from jealousy or a fear of losing me. It had just been the two of us for so long. Sure, we'd both had long-term partners but never anything as permanent as a proposal. I tried to reassure her I'd always be there for her but it wasn't enough to get her to drop her animosity towards him.

Chris used to get so frustrated with how much effort I still made with her despite her reservations about our relationship. Telling me she didn't deserve my support when she didn't reciprocate it. He was an only child though, and didn't understand the bond that siblings share. I can still remember the last argument I had with him.

Andrew had called me out of the blue to let me know Isabella was struggling. She was falling behind in the polls, and Marcus had left her. Of course, I raced upstairs and packed an overnight bag whilst finishing our conversation. I promised Andrew I'd be on the next train across. It's one of the few times the two of us have been in sync, united by a shared passion to protect Isabella.

Chris had followed me up the stairs, standing in the doorway like a storm cloud waiting to erupt. We were supposed to be hosting his parents for dinner. It had been planned for months and had taken a lot of difficult conversations to organise.

His dad was due to move into a care home because his dementia was progressing and Chris wanted one family meal together before it was too late. A chance for the three of them to bury the ghosts that had kept them apart for much of Chris' life.

Yes, I realise now that I should have stayed. Chris was supposed to be the family I'd chosen, and therefore, so were his parents. His worries and concerns should have been mine, and I knew what a big deal seeing his parents was for him. They hadn't gotten together in years.

But I chose Isabella. I sidelined him once again. And whilst he followed me down the stairs, shouting out all manner of accusations that even then I knew to be true, I told him it was just something he had to get used to. Isabella was my younger sister and I would always be there if she needed me.

When I returned home after a week of unanswered texts he was gone without a trace. I'd just put his silence down to sulking. I never imagined I'd lose him over my relationship with Isabella. We were supposed to get married and start a life together. A life that was ripped away from me. Having my heart shattered so completely made me guard it more fiercely.

I was wary of new people and their intentions. Which is why my lip had sneered last night as I watched the Inspector hold the door open for my sister. She'd smiled up at him and then they'd briefly brushed against each other whilst entering the restaurant. Like two lovers on a shy first date.

A professional wouldn't behave like that - which meant that this man wasn't a professional. And if he wasn't a professional, he had no business in protecting my sister from a perceived threat. Granted, I was the one behind the so-called threat, but he didn't know that. He didn't know that she wasn't in any danger. And here he was, using her moment of vulnerability to swoop in and take advantage.

Was he intending to ride on her political coattails to a promotion for himself? Or did he fancy a cushy life as the husband of the future Prime Minister? Was she just a meal ticket to him?

All of these questions and more were running through my mind as Andrew regarded me, waiting for an answer to a question that hadn't broken through my thoughts.

"Sorry?" I asked.

He let out a huff of air from his nose, a sign he was controlling his temper around me. It's nice to know he finds my presence as grating as I find his.

"I said Isabella has asked me to book you a room at the Hilton nearby. She'll be by as soon as she can."

So, my sister wasn't planning on dropping everything to see me. She hadn't even come downstairs to greet me - sending her little errand boy to take care of it. Never mind. She's very busy. I shouldn't have expected otherwise.

And yet I did.

I had hoped at least.

"That's very kind of her." I stop short of thanking him for his help in securing the room for me. It may be petty, and not entirely his fault, but Isabella's snub has rubbed me up the wrong way. Surely she could have spared me two minutes to deliver the news herself?

"It's under your name. She's charged it to her personal card so, May, don't take the piss." He makes sure to open the meeting room door as he delivers the last part of his sentence. Hoping for his words to carry to some unsuspecting parties' ears, for gossip to spread about me and what I might have done previously to earn such a warning.

In truth, I always behave immaculately when it comes to Isabella's reputation. I'm never caught stumbling around drunk outside my own home. I always make sure to mind my manners - all too aware that my behaviour could reflect on her should it be captured by the wrong people. Of course, the papers had called me over the years, hoping to find a family axe they could grind to extract some gossip from me. But I'd never do that to her. I'd never betray her like that. I'm better than that.

Andrew's shadow is lurking outside the door. He obviously expected to escort me from the premises but my coffee has just brewed and I don't feel like leaving yet, so I pick up my mug, sink into an armchair, and take a sip. Andrew couldn't openly throw me out. My sister is his soon-to-be party leader. He can't force me to do anything. I outrank him in her court and I intend to enjoy that fact.

He scowls at me but doesn't say anymore, the silence as the door closes behind him says all it needs to.

Chapter Five - Isabella

May's arrival has put a bit of a damper on my plans. I was hoping to invite Inspector Coulson - James, out for a drink tonight. We had such a lovely time together at dinner yesterday. Conversation had been easy and a smile had never been far from my face.

He was charm personified and I know he found my company enjoyable too. He never let his deep brown eyes stray too far from mine the entire time we were together. I didn't want to look desperate by inviting him out again so soon, but I also didn't want to risk him losing interest, or for him only appearing in my life in a professional capacity. I had to make sure he saw me as more than a case.

I had been composing a text to him when my office phone had rung to let me know May was waiting downstairs. I quickly sent her a message; she was a little high maintenance if she felt she wasn't being appreciated, and then contacted Andrew. He had a room booked for her at the nearby Hilton before I even finished explaining what was going on. He knew what a wild card May could be. We couldn't risk her causing any drama in the building. The walls have ears after all.

So now I find myself at a crossroads about my evening plans. I should go and have dinner with my sister. Of course I should. That's the only real option.

But the pull to see James is so strong. Already he's the person I want to share all the mundane details of my day with. If this relationship became something permanent, that would be positive for me both personally and professionally. I'd gain a partner who made me laugh, and my constituents would gain a party leader who knew how to marry well.

I have to resist though, I know I do. At least whilst May is here. I have no idea how long she's planning to stay, and I know that to ask her that would only cause offence. So I must play the doting younger sister and entertain her as much as my schedule allows. As I pull on my coat I feel a wave of guilt descend on me. It's unkind to think of May in terms of a duty to perform. She's my sister and I love her. She's just been a lot of work the last few years, ever since Chris.

Chris.

Bloody Chris.

Nevertheless, she is my sister. No matter how much stress she causes me. I can give her a few evenings of my time easily enough. If James is worth all I think he is, then he will be patient. He will understand that family has to come first. At least sometimes.

"May," I said down the phone at the end of my working day. "I'm on my way to collect you. I've booked a table at a lovely Indian restaurant." It's her voicemail. I don't bother introducing myself in my message, she'd know who I was even without caller ID. Our voices are second nature to the other.

Throwing the security guard a wave as I walk out of the doors, I'm grateful I picked up my scarf from the back of my office door. It might clash with the royal red of my coat but it's cosy and comforting. My old secretary knitted it for me. It makes me feel warm and loved, As though she put all her feelings for me into the yarn.

I can still picture her, sitting behind her desk, patiently clicking the needles together as she created something out of nothing. Agatha had been with me since I first started campaigning to be an MP. She'd watched me grow through the ranks and had a scrapbook that was bursting at the seams of my press clippings. She was like the grandmother I'd never known and it broke my heart, genuinely, when I had to make the tough call to let her go.

But as she aged, her grasp on confidentiality lessened until she was too much of a liability for even my emotional connection to keep her in a job. She cried in our very last meeting, I've never felt so guilty. Thankfully, Andrew had been waiting just outside the room, ready to tidy up behind her so I didn't have to spend a moment longer dwelling on my decision. I've let a lot of people go throughout my career, but Agatha, still to this day, stung the most.

Before I know it I'm standing in the reception of the Hilton when my phone beeps to let me know of an incoming message. Like a giddy school girl, I desperately hope it's James but my stomach stiffens as I see an unknown number on my screen. I don't want to swipe and open this message, I want it to disappear from existence.

Not many things in life knock me off balance but these messages were beginning to. I thought we got it right when I assumed it was one of the ex-staffers, but the arrival of a new message proved that I jumped to the wrong conclusion. I must let Andrew know sooner rather than later.

How long is May staying in town?

It feels as though my phone has leapt six feet into the air out of my grasp when in reality my fingers just lost their grip. It clatters to the floor and everyone in the quiet reception area turns around to look at me.

Don't recognise me.

Please don't recognise me.

God, I wish I wasn't wearing this coat. It's like an attention beacon right now. Usually, I'm beyond proud to wear my parties colour but right now I wish I was a shadow in the corner of a room, completely unnoticed. With a nervous chuckle for my audience, I bend down and pick up the phone before making a beeline for the bar. May can come and meet me here.

May.

The person behind these messages knows she's in town. Which means they've been watching me, or her. Anger replaces fear, how dare they try to intimidate me like this? When I find whoever's responsible for this I will make sure they regret their decision to toy with me.

May can be a bit of a handful at times but she's my sister, the only family I have left, and I'm not about to let anything happen to her.

My first instinct is to call her and demand she hop on a train back to her home, order her to lock the doors and stay hunkered down in her bed. There are two problems with that plan, though.

May would never listen to my instructions and it would mean whoever just sent me that message would have won- that I would have let them scare me into changing my life and plans.

Picking up my phone I dial May's number again, making sure to fix a smile on my face in case the perpetrator is watching. I fight the urge to frantically check my surroundings, because what would I be looking for? A man in a macintosh with a comedy beard? No. I must play it cool. I mustn't become ruffled.

"Hey, I'm just downstairs in the bar," I say, barely listening to her response as I give in to my base instincts and scout the area around me. A nondescript businessman hunches over his laptop and a mum is trying to convince her teenage son to put down his phone and talk to her - there's nobody I'm concerned about in here.

"Okay, see you in a bit." I hang up the phone and signal for the waiter to come over. "Could I have two glasses of white please?" I flash him one of my best smiles. It never hurts to leave a good impression after all, and as he busies himself with the copper measure and two glasses I type out a quick message to James.

I've received another message. Are you free tomorrow to discuss?

One silver lining of this latest threat - it's given me a reason to keep the Inspector in my life a little longer. Not that I intended on letting him slip out of it when the case was solved, but now I have an excuse to keep in touch that doesn't make me seem too keen.

The waiter places the glasses on the bar in front of me and I pull a few notes from my purse, making sure to wave away his offer of change. It's amazing the little gestures one can undertake to gain favour with people, and I know I've been generous enough with my tip that he'll tell his friends. I hear the distinctive stomp of May's heels on the wooden floor and look up towards her with a genuine smile.

My big sister. My beautiful and yet broken big sister. Losing Chris did a number on her I hadn't expected. She used to be the life and soul of every room she walked into, somebody everybody wanted and needed to talk to. Now it's as though she's shrunk two feet.

She's lost so much weight her skin is drawn tight around her bones and although her cheeks have amazing structure, I preferred it when she didn't look like a model from the nineties. Sometimes I wonder how much responsibility has to sit at my door for what happened to May, but my days are so busy I can't dwell on it perhaps as much as I should.

She scans the room until she finds my face and returns my smile. I nod at the glasses of wine in front of me and relief floods her features. She must have had a long week too. Sometimes I forget that May has a life and problems of her own and that everything doesn't revolve around me and my political wish list. I really must make more of an effort to be there for her.

But then my phone beeps, an incoming call from James, and once again I put my own life ahead of hers.

Chapter Six - May

I truly believed that dropping my name into the latest message would get Isabella to pay attention. And I suppose the fact that she told the Inspector about it meant she'd taken it seriously, but still, she didn't prioritise me.

She answered that damn phone just as I was walking towards her, leaving me to awkwardly perch on a bar stool at her side, nursing my glass of wine. I tried to act like I didn't care about her phone call but there wasn't much else to occupy my time with so I ended up openly eavesdropping.

"You can't be serious?" She asks the caller, her hand flying up to her mouth in shock. I reach over and place my hand on the small of her back, whatever is happening is bad news and all the resentment I had festering towards her disappears. She doesn't shrug me off, instead, she looks towards me, her eyes wide and brimming with tears.

"What's happening?" I mouth to her as she listens to the voice at the other end of the phone. She gives a quick shake of her head, a way to let me know she needs to focus right now. For once I don't mind her dismissal, whatever news she's just been given is more serious than my petty need for her attention.

"When? Right. Okay. Okay. Well, thanks for letting me know. No, I'll be okay. I'm with my sister." Only hearing one side of a conversation can be difficult but hearing those last few words makes me happy - she will be okay - because she is with me. I'll be sure of it.

I wait as she hangs up the phone and takes a deep breath, giving her the chance to centre her emotions.

"Do you remember Samantha Stokes?" she asks, and I ponder the name for a while before a face surfaces from my memory. Samantha Stokes had been Isabella's school friend when she was eleven years old, the two of them had been inseparable since meeting on the first day of term and being assigned to the same tutor group.

They walked to school together every morning and spent most evenings together as well. My dad used to call them the gruesome twosome to elicit obnoxious groans from them both. He always liked to poke the bear, did Dad.

Or at least they'd been super close until…

Until…

I can't quite remember what happened between the two of them, but I know it had been bad. I can hear the wisps of an argument just out of reach of my memory.

"She's dead," finishes Isabella without waiting for me to confirm I even remember the girl.

"Oh God, I'm so sorry, Bella." She must be in a state as she lets my use of her childhood name slide. I haven't dared to use it since she gave me cold shoulder to let me know exactly how much she didn't appreciate it. That had been a rough year. Like a dog though, I eventually learnt that bad behaviour could not be rewarded.

"James found out from one of his colleagues. It looks like she overdosed." The colour has drained from her face and I keep my hand tightly in the small of her back, worried she might fall from the stool in shock. Even though we'd never mentioned Samantha since that night all those years ago, I know the girl had meant a lot to Isabella.

It must be hard to lose a large part of your childhood no matter the distance you've put between it.

"Did James," we should refer to him as Inspector Coulson but I let it pass, "mention if they'd caught whoever supplied the drugs?"

"No, they haven't." With a small shake of her head, she leans forward in her stool and picks up her glass of wine, clutching it in her palm, drawing strength from it. "Do you mind if we miss dinner tonight? Maybe just have a drink here? I don't feel like being in a crowd right now."

"Of course, let's get a table," I reply and she smiles at me. I'm transported back to the day our parents died. The way she looked up at me and expected me to fix everything, to repair what was so impossibly broken. I failed her back then, lost sight of my sanity, and lost my grip on her safety. I won't do that again.

"Do you mind grabbing some more drinks? I'm just going to sit down." Not waiting for my response she empties her glass down her throat, places it delicately back on the bar and totters over to a table at the back of the room. One that's semi-concealed compared to the others.

I've always been proud of my sister's ability to keep her head above water no matter the situation and I know that tonight will be no different. Of course, she will confide in me, I'm her sister, but should any members of the public interrupt us tonight, I know she'll hold it together.

She'll paint on the smile that won her a landslide of votes in the local election and they will be none the wiser as to what she's just been told. Honestly, it's a life skill to be able to detach that completely from your emotions. I wish I was more like her.

I've always been too emotional. I've been told that by everybody in my life from my family through to my lovers. I can't help myself though. It's like my emotions are on autopilot and I have no control over where they take me.

There was this one night, back when I was about fourteen and Isabella had gotten into trouble. And I mean really gotten into trouble. My father had shouted at her, which was unheard of as she could rarely do wrong in his eyes.

My mother had tried to calm him by explaining that Isabella had merely fallen in with the wrong crowd, that she wasn't a bad kid, just a good one who had made a poor decision. I'd been peering through the bannisters at the top of the stairs, watching the drama unfold in the living room. A knock at the door had startled me and I'd leapt further back into the shadows.

There was a very serious-looking police officer at the door. He greeted my father by name, and it was clear that they were drinking buddies from the familiarity between them. I heard the officer mention Samantha's name before he closed the living room door behind him, and that's the last thing I remember.

It was pitch black when my father's shadow loomed over me and he carried me to bed. In the morning, around breakfast, it was like last night had never happened. There was no animosity between Isabella and my parents, and I assumed whatever had caused such drama between them had been resolved whilst I slept.

Carrying a fresh bottle of white and two glasses over to where Isabella was sitting, I'm struck by the fact that's the last time I can remember Samantha's name being mentioned in our home.

"How are you doing?" I ask as I sit opposite her. She's never been one for overt displays of physical affection. So even though I'd prefer to sit by her side in the booth and place my arm around her shoulder, I hold back on my natural instincts and do as she would wish. As I always have.

"I'm okay, just a bit shaken up. It's not news you ever expect to hear, is it?"

"No, I suppose it's not. Here." I pour her a generous glass of wine and she lifts it gratefully.

"Thanks. To Samantha, I suppose." She raises her glass slightly and I follow suit, joining in with her half-hearted toast.

"Whatever happened between the two of you anyway?" I ask a question I know I shouldn't, and her face clouds over. My sister isn't the biggest fan of talking about the past. She calls it wallowing and avoids it wherever she can.

"We just drifted apart, the way childhood friendships do."

That isn't true though. I know that isn't true. Their friendship ended abruptly, that much I can remember.

One night they were inseparable, then the next morning they were strangers. We never spoke about the girl or the memories we shared with her, ever again. I want to press Isabella, to explain to her about the gaps in my memory, and hope she gives me the truth, but I daren't.

She's emotionally fragile right now and that makes her volatile. I've been on the receiving end of my sister's temper before and I didn't want to risk it again. My sister never talks about things she doesn't wish to.

It's what makes her such an excellent politician.

Not once in her career, nay, in her entire life, has my sister uttered a word accidentally. Everything she says and does is planned to ensure the best possible outcome. She's a publicist's dream.

"James is worried that there might be a link with the notes. He doesn't believe her overdose was accidental" she says.

Now's the time for me to confess that I'm the mystery sender. That I did it all just to keep her safe in a roundabout sort of way. I should tell her the truth, so she knows she has nothing to fear despite Samantha's death.

But I can't.

If I tell her then I don't know how she'll react, and I can't risk losing her right now. I have to get my head straight before I tell her, otherwise, I might end up back in the Sanctuary if I can't cope with her reaction.

"I'm sure it's not. Nobody would have a reason to link you to Samantha." That's the best reassurance I can give her.

"May, I have to tell you something," she stares into her glass of wine before fixing her eyes on me. Her eye contact is intense and I brace myself for what's coming next. "I had a message before you came down, whoever's sending me these notes knows you're in town. They mentioned it."

I wish the ground would swallow me whole. What kind of person puts their sister through this level of mental torture? How sick and twisted do I have to be to have even dreamt up this plan, let alone followed through on it?

I can no longer remember why I even decided to undertake it in the first place. Yes, of course, I was worried about her safety. But I always have been. And why did I choose those words:

'I know what you did'

When I know full well that my sister is an open book?

None of this makes sense to me anymore. Oh God, I hope I'm not completely losing my mind. The last time I had gaps in my memory like this… No. I don't want to think about that time. I'd rather forget that time.

"Well of course they did. That makes complete sense." She looks shocked at how easily I've taken this news. "If it's ex-staffers like you suspect then they're bound to still have friends inside your building. How else would somebody know I've come to visit?"

My reassurance sounds hollow to my ears, but that's because I know it's all a fabrication. Thankfully though, it appears to calm her somewhat.

"You're right. Of course, you're right. I'm still going to show the message to James, just in case."

"That sounds sensible to me." I keep my voice cool but my nerves are so frayed I'm worried they'll start shooting out of my eyes. What if the Inspector can link the burner phone back to me? Sure, the kid who sold it to me promised discretion, but that was before he had a member of the law knocking on his door. I need to stay calm. If I stay calm, then I'll stay in control.

We sit and drink our wine in comfortable silence for a few minutes before a member of staff approaches our table. A switch flicks on inside my sister and she practically glows as she talks to them about policies and current events. Eventually, the young server leaves and Isabella's mood slips into something quieter, more reflective.

"Have you heard any more about Marcus' case?" I ask, searching for a topic that will drag us away from the messages I've been sending. The less we talk about that the better.

"No. But I wasn't close enough to him to warrant regular updates." Her tone is cold and flat and I can't tell if it's because she doesn't care or if she cares more than she wants to admit. I can still remember the hollow sobs that shook her entire body on the day he left her. She'd truly loved him, trusted him, and he'd turned and walked away as though she were nothing. I haven't been that angry at someone in a very long time.

"It's okay to be sad about it, you know. He was a very important part of your life. Samantha too." Sometimes I have to let Isabella know that it's okay to be human and show weakness.

"Oh, I know. But it doesn't feel right to grieve for somebody you no longer know. Not properly anyway."

She gazes down into her now empty wine glass and I know my window of time with my sister is drawing to an end. I briefly consider suggesting another bottle but I know she'll turn me down.

She's a solitary creature away from her profession and she'll want to go home and recentre before the madness starts over tomorrow.

"Right, I'm going to make a move if that's okay. I'm sorry again about dinner. Order whatever you like and put it on the room. I'll make sure to clear it tomorrow." She leans over the table and squeezes my hand, one of the only signs of physical affection she can openly tolerate. "Thank you again for coming to see me, I didn't realise how much I needed to see a friendly face."

With a brief wave over her shoulder, she disappears from the bar, her red coat flapping in the breeze she creates with her tempo. My sister is going to change the world one day, of that I'm certain.

I need to stop messing with her head, to stop being so selfish. I truly want only the best for her, I do. When I get up to my room I'm going to run all the burner phones under the tap and make sure I can never use them again. This madness ends now.

Chapter Seven - Isabella

"I really think you need to start taking this more seriously." James' voice is firm, and if I didn't find him so attractive I'd be irritated at his tone.

Thankfully for him though there's plenty about him to visually distract me from my simmering resentment. His brown eyes so dark they could be pools of midnight, ready for me to dive in and drown. The upper muscles in his arms that strain and stretch beneath the crisp white cotton of his shirt. Or the perfectly styled pathway of his beard that creeps up to his ears that I long to breathe heavily into. Yes, there was plenty about James that could keep me occupied.

However, I've been sat in my office with the Inspector and Andrew for the last twenty minutes and still neither of them have listened to a word I've said. My patience is beginning to wear so thin that no amount of visual stimulation can soothe it.

They don't understand that I am taking the notes seriously, or at least I am now that my sister has been brought into them. Prior to that, I must admit I hadn't given them as much concern as perhaps I should have done, quick to dismiss them as nothing more than an ex-staff members prank. Now they've made mention of May though, now it's personal, now I'm listening.

My sister is the one person who actually matters to me, who I actually owe something to. It's been just the two of us against the world for so long and I can't let her get hurt because someone has an axe to grind against me. Despite the new level of seriousness I feel towards this anonymous threat, I know that the notes and the death of Samantha are not linked.

Samantha was a troublemaker when we were younger. It's why my parents stopped us from spending so much time together. I'll admit - I got wrapped up in her, I made some bad decisions because I wanted to impress her but thankfully my parents made sure it all went away.

I was lucky that back then, at least, they were people I could rely on. People who actually put me at the forefront of their thoughts and actions, didn't last forever though did it? Eventually they let me down. Most people do.

It wouldn't surprise me if James gets a call to say a small time so-and-so had been hauled into custody on supplying the drugs that killed Samantha. It was inevitable that one day she would go too far and piss off the wrong person, anybody who knew her can testify to that.

Then maybe he'll finally listen to me that the two cases are not interlinked, because for now he's adamant that they are. He's actually trying to convince me to hire security guards to shadow me for a few days. It would be a waste of money and resources.

How does he not see that it's not myself I'm worried about, it's my sister? This isn't my first time swimming with sharks and I have plenty of friends I could call on should somebody step too far out of line but May doesn't. May only has me.

It's my job to keep her sheltered from my work. She's still too fragile since losing Chris. Her time in the Sanctuary hadn't worked as well as it had after we lost our parents. I don't want to lose my grip on my sister, nor do I want her to lose her grip on reality.

Andrew has been surprisingly quiet throughout James' lecture about personal safety which is irritating as

I know he's on my side in this argument. If I'm certain the two aren't interlinked then he is as well. We're symbiotic like that.

"How about if May comes to stay with me?" It's as close to a compromise as I'm willing to step. At least then he wouldn't be able to lament about the dangers of me rattling around my house alone at night.

I mean, sure, I kind of hoped he'd offer to come and protect me from things that go bump in the dark, but he hadn't, so I have to make my own plans.

"I'm not sure May is best equipped to protect you should she need to," interjects Andrew. Trust him to choose this moment to find his voice.

"I'm perfectly capable of protecting myself, thank you." I resist the urge to flex my muscles, now isn't the time for humour. "Besides, as I keep telling you, the notes have nothing to do with Samantha's death."

"What about Marcus?" asks James, and I have to hold in an audible sigh.

"Nor his. They are two completely separate tragedies and whilst yes, I knew both victims, their deaths had nothing to do with me. Just a case of the wrong person, wrong time."

"How about if I came to stay instead?" offers Andrew and I see James' face cloud over.

Andrew is an attractive man, that I can't deny. His face is well structured and his shoulders hold the rest of his body well. But there's never been even a whisper of a crush between us, which people often find hard to believe but it is the truth.

True, there was a connection between the two of us when we first met, but it was spiritual rather than physical. A sense that I'd met another piece of my soul, somebody who was on the same path that I was, and who would support me and my dreams no matter what.

As soon as his informal interview in the student

union cafe finished, I cancelled all the other applicants. There was no point in wasting my time when I'd already met the campaign manager of my dreams.

We've worked together for nearly a decade now and his loyalty is as unfaltering now as it was on his first day when he arrived fresh eyed and bushy-tailed. He truly believes I will one day be Prime Minister and that together we will change the country. So I'm not surprised that he's willing to come and sleep on my sofa to save me the awkwardness of sharing a home with my sister.

It's not that I don't love May, I truly do. It's that I can't quite be my complete and honest self around her, and it's going to be hard to keep a mask on twenty four hours a day whilst she's under my roof. Andrew knows me, warts and all, and accepts me for who I am. So of course he's stepping up to bat, offering to go above and beyond for my benefit once again.

"Probably not the best idea given the way walls talk," I reply, smiling at him gratefully as I do so. The rumour mill loves to paint a relationship between the two of us if we even go out to eat lunch together. I can't imagine what they'd say if we started to have platonic sleepovers. I'm not about to give the gossip hags more ammunition to bring me down.

James looks momentarily relieved that I've turned Andrew's company down, but he tries to hide it behind a gruff cough. Even jealousy looks attractive on him. If Andrew weren't here I'd definitely suggest that he stay the night with me - but I know exactly what my campaign manager's reaction would be.

He would shut the idea down before the sentence has even finished leaving my lips, and he would be right to. I don't have overnight guests at my house anymore, there's too much chance that they could go poking around and find something I'd rather they didn't. As

Marcus proved, nobody is above a kiss and tell. Plus the press would have a field day with the photographs. We might live in more modern times but words like 'slag' and 'slut' are never too far from people's vocabulary where a woman's sexuality is concerned.

Instead, when the mood strikes, I take my guests to a hotel room. Andrew books the room we use and a meeting room as a cover, his excuse should anyone ask is the hotel room gives him somewhere private to unwind whilst I undertake my meetings. Then I wait for my date to arrive, take care of business and they leave. And that's been enough for me for a long time.

I don't think it would be enough with James though.

I can already tell I want more than a snatched afternoon of delight with the Inspector. Perhaps it's the thrill of playing with fire that's igniting these feelings within me, but whatever it is, I know I want more than just a few hours with him. Maybe even more than a few days. It's looking more and more likely though that all those fantasies will have to take a backseat until we get to the bottom of whose sending me notes.

I know what you did.

They keep repeating. A little derivative for my taste but I'm sure it would make a lesser woman worry. Not me though. I know how deeply my secrets are buried and how improbable it would be for them to be discovered. I have, after all, wanted a career in politics since I was about thirteen and I've lived my life carefully with that always in mind.

Any skeletons in my closet are nothing more than dust by now. And thanks to Andrew we always have a contingency should any try to rear their heads and dampen my reputation. I'm the politician people actually trust, a first if you ask me, my popularity ebbs out across many parties - not just my own.

People who had never considered voting red before have confidently agreed that I'm the best bottom for the top seat - a headline the papers gleefully ran with. Now that bit of gossip I didn't mind. What woman doesn't want to be told she has a nice arse?

May probably. May would hate being objectified, would hate being the centre of attention for something so tawdry. It's one of the reasons I'd been so taken back when she'd called to let me know she was engaged to Chris.

An engagement would lead to a wedding and a wedding very much involves everyone looking at the bride. Maybe in all the excitement she'd forgotten about that part, she just sounded so joyful that somebody loved her enough to promise her forever.

He hadn't been for forever though, he'd just been a ship passing through. He was never good enough to become family - he proved that in the end.

"Decision made then. May will come and stay with me for a few days," I say.

"Shouldn't we check that she's happy about this?" asks Andrew and I get the feeling he's stalling for time or at the very least he's trying to plant some seeds of doubt about my plan into the Inspector's head.

There's nothing to worry about though. My sister is one of the few people in the world I can trust. It's not like she's going to go rooting through my drawers to find a story to sell. She's proved her loyalty to me over and over again throughout our lives. May will always have my best interests in mind.

"She'll be fine." I shut him down with a look I hope James misses, as it's not a pleasant one.

"I'm sure she'll be pleased to spend some time with you," James interrupts our back and forth and his voice calms me down.

I was quickly growing irritated at Andrew's interruption. Clearly he thought that his staying at my house was the only sensible solution and he wasn't ready to back down from that. I've noticed that over the last few weeks Andrew's backbone was growing and he was beginning to behave as though he always knew what was best for me.

I wasn't used to this change in his personality. He'd always been more of a follower than a leader. I'll have to have a private word with him soon about it, to make sure he remembers who's truly in charge.

"Thank you for your time Inspector Coulson. I'm afraid Isabella has a two o'clock so we'll have to draw this meeting to a close," says Andrew.

I bristle even though I know he is right. My press officer has asked for a meeting with me and I really can't cancel it, not with everything that's going on right now. But still, Andrew didn't have to be so abrupt.

"Of course, Isabella you have my number if you need me." And with those parting words James leaves my office. I feel a strong pull towards him, I'm trying to remember if I'd felt like this about Marcus when we'd first met. Or is this what a real connection feels like?

I turn to face Andrew. We have fifteen minutes before my appointment and I have a few things I need to get off my chest.

"Andrew," I begin, "I believe the two of us need to have a little talk."

Chapter Eight - May

Living with Isabella, sorry - staying with Isabella, is more than I could have hoped for when I began this little descent into madness.

We haven't shared a roof long-term since she left to go to university. I've missed the noise and chaos her presence brings. The never-ending phone calls, constant channel hopping, and the clicking of heels on laminate flooring. It's like a trip down memory lane and I'm soaking up every minute of it.

I'm not delusional.

I know eventually she'll tire of my presence, realise I'm not in any real danger and ask me to leave. But until that point in time, I'm going to drink up every hour we get to spend together. I'm more relaxed than I've been in the years since Chris left. Maybe I'm just not built to live alone anymore.

When I came out of the Sanctuary back then, Isabella had commented on how healthy I looked. Well rested was the term she used, in fact, and I suppose given I'd spent three months having my every need taken care of that should have been the case.

It wasn't though.

Isabella had meant only the best for me when she paid for me to be privately sectioned at the Sanctuary, I know it had been her only option in the face of my mental breakdown.

I'd begun flinging the most awful accusations at her, making threats that turn my skin to ice when I look back on them. She thinks I don't remember that time in my life but I do remember parts. I think about them constantly.

Looking back on that time all I ever see is blood. Pints and pints of blood all over the floor, the walls and seeping into my skin. I try my best not to look back too deeply into the past, something my therapist agrees with. Growing up I never thought I'd be someone who ended up with a therapist, and yet here I am.

Another gift from my sister. A way to keep me stable. And this is how I repay all of her kindness and support. By sending her threatening notes and causing her undue panic? I'm a terrible person and I need to confess.

But if I confess then there is a chance that all the love she has for me will vanish. That she'll be so disgusted with me she'll cut ties. Or worse. Send me back to the Sanctuary. I can't go back there. I won't. All I can do is stop playing this game. Accept I'm sometimes going to be second fiddle in my little sister's life and move on.

That's the natural order of things anyway. We break away from our familial ties, grow our independence, and find our chosen family. It's just a shame that the one she's chosen includes Andrew.

As though summoned by my thoughts, there's a knock at the door. Before I can stand from my seat I hear the front door unlock and in he walks. Andrew. With that smug smile on his face.

"Oh, I'd forgotten you were still here," he says, glancing his eyes over me as though I'm nothing but an inconvenience in his morning.

"No, you hadn't." I'm not about to waste even a minute of my day playing Andrews games. "Isabella chose me, remember?"

I know it's petty. I know it is. But I can't resist reminding him that he was the lesser choice when push came to shove. Because I know he would have offered to come and stay with her.

I know it in the same way I know the sky is blue. And yet, she chose me. For a moment he's lost for a retort. I watch as his lip curls up into a sneer and his fingers begin to draw into his palm.

"Isabella!" he calls. "The town car is here." Without speaking another word to me he stalks out of the front door, slamming it behind him. The sound thrills me. I've finally gotten to him, after all these years, I've finally managed to push his buttons and cause him to lose control.

My sister walks gracefully down the stairs, as though she's Cinderella arriving at the ball, and once again I'm taken aback by her composure and beauty.

She looks just like our mum did at that age. I kept the old family photo albums after we sold mum and dad's house, and I look at them far more regularly than I should.

My mother had been a beautiful woman, with her shoulder length dark curls and twinkling green eyes. Isabella really is the spit of her. Which is something I'd never say out loud. Isabella doesn't like to talk about our parents. She says it's too painful to remember.

I disagree.

I ache to talk about our shared past, to reminisce about the good times the four of us had together. The laughs around the dinner table. The private jokes and jests that held us all together. We had a very blessed childhood, and for the life of me, I don't understand why she doesn't want to recognise that. But, as always, I respect her decision on the matter.

"Are you sure you don't want to come in with me today?" she asks, and I want to say yes. I want to spend as much time with her as possible before I inevitably tell her the truth about the messages. Because despite knowing all that will come after I do, I know that I have to. I have always been honest with my sister. Eventually.

"No honestly, I'll be okay here. I'm just going to watch some television and catch up on a few emails." I gesture at my laptop bag. "It'll be tax filing season soon and it's going to be mind-numbing, so I intend to enjoy every day up until then as much as possible." She laughs as though I've told a joke, and I don't think I have but I smile at her anyway.

"I'll have Andrew pick up your prescription then. Saves you popping out." She's such a considerate person, wanting to make sure I don't run out of the anti-depressants that keep me more stable than not. My heart swells ten sizes under her care. With a quick hug, she's off and out of the door and I have a whole empty day ahead of me.

I am always honest with my sister. To a point.

There are no emails to answer because I'm on sabbatical. I called yesterday when I was alone and told the office I needed some annual leave. Of course, they agreed straight away, I've built up enough goodwill over the time I've worked for them that they rarely question what I do.

My brain isn't really in gear as I find myself climbing up the steps towards Isabella's bedroom. And it's definitely unplugged as I open the door and walk inside my sister's bedroom. There's a voice whispering in my ear that something in this room will help me understand her better, will help me see beyond the walls she's built up around herself over the years.

Sometimes it feels like the girl I grew up alongside disappeared at the same time we lost our parents. I was eighteen that night and she was just fifteen. It had been her birthday a few weeks prior.

Up until then, she'd been a bubbly bright thing - always looking for a way to make people laugh or for a mystery to dig her teeth into. But the night they died all of that changed. With a snap of a finger and a crash of a car, I lost any resemblance of the family I'd always had.

It's why I'd clung on so hard to her after it happened, why I made her defer her university placement until she was nineteen. I was so sure that what had happened to her personality was just a mixture of shock and grief that I wanted to be there for her when it passed. It never did though. She's remained aloof and locked off ever since.

Now is my chance to work out why.

So, once again, I find myself making a morally grey decision under the guise of caring for my sister. Her mattress is soft under me as I sit on it, pausing for a minute to take in my surroundings. Unlike the guest room I'm staying in there are no generic canvases or black-and-white photographs scattered artfully on the walls. No vase of fresh flowers on the dresser and certainly no hand-stitched comforter on the foot of the bed.

No, Isabella's room had none of those homely touches. Her white, and they were white, not an eggshell in sight, walls were stark and bare. Her grey-stained oak furniture was empty, with no signs of clutter. Not even a hairbrush kept the mirror on the dressing table company. It was as though nobody lived in this room. There was no personality to tell me otherwise.

Which was strange because the rest of her home was decorated aesthetically, and every room came across as warm and welcoming. And yet this room, the one room that was just for her, was barren. Was this the real Isabella? Was this the side of my sister she hides away from the world behind smiles and throw pillows? And if that's the case, if this is a glimpse inside her real and raw personality - why does she feel she can't trust me with it?

I'd love her regardless. She should know that by now.

I must admit, I can see why she hasn't decorated the home with this level of extreme minimalism - I feel like I'm in a hospital room. It's uncomfortable to sit here for too long.

To distract myself from the suffocating blankness of the room around me I shuffle up the bed until my leg is resting against her bedside table.

I really shouldn't be edging towards this handle.

I definitely shouldn't be pulling it open.

And I certainly shouldn't be peeking inside.

There's a glimmer of excitement working its way up my back as I pull the drawer further out. It's the thrill of being caught doing something I shouldn't. We all enjoy that sensation, even if we won't admit to it. I bet it comes from childhood, from the first time we told a fib - it's the magical sense of making the unbelievable true. It's unbelievable that I'm rummaging in my sister's private belongings and yet it's also true.

For the briefest of moments, I worry about what I might find. After all, I know the sort of items a single person keeps in their bedside drawers. I myself have two in fact. But, I decide, if I happen upon a sex toy or three I'll just bleach my hands and forget it ever happened. I'm quite good at repressing things like that.

Now the drawer is open I'm mildly disappointed to just find a few belongings. A discarded paperback novel that looks as though it's never been opened. A remote control for a television that doesn't exist in this room. A blank notebook and a biro.

It's all as bland as the room I'm sitting in. As I go to close the drawer with a sigh though, I find it's jammed. With the lightest sense of panic creeping in I wedge my hand into the remaining opening and shuffle it backwards until it can go no further. There's something at the back of the drawer that's fallen into the cabinet itself, preventing me from opening or closing it, providing evidence of my curiosity.

I can't have that.

I swear at myself as the wooden edges of the drawer rub against my skin but I have no choice. I have to move whatever is causing this block so Isabella doesn't know I've been in here. Finally, my hand finds a string and I give it a hard tug which does the job. I can move the drawer again.

Pulling the string out of the opening I hold a small white cotton bag in my hand. I know this bag.

I don't want to open this bag.

In this bag is my engagement ring from Chris. I know that because I gave it to Isabella right before I was sent to the Sanctuary. I told her to get rid of it. And yet here it is.

Taking a deep breath I open the bag and turn it upside down onto the bed. The ring falls out and I stare at it, surprised at the emotions that swell out of me.

Grief. Pure, unfiltered grief at the sight of it.

We would have been married by now. Would have been settling into our lives together. If only, if only, if only…

I shove the ring back into the bag alongside the other small trinkets that keep it company. A pair of cufflinks and a hair tie that's seen better days. And a rusty locket from a necklace. My fingers edge towards the locket, wanting to open the clasp and look inside despite the way my brain is screaming at me to stop.

Before I can look though the silence in the room around me is rudely interrupted by the harsh ring of my mobile phone. I drop the locket into the bag unopened and shove it back inside the drawer, slamming it to a close before I draw a breath and answer my phone.

Chapter Nine - Isabella

It took May five rings before she answered, which was incredibly unusual. It was just enough time to allow the threads of worry to lay seed in my mind. What if whoever was behind the notes had managed to bypass the security alarms at my house and get to her? How would I cope if I had to say goodbye to my big sister, my protector?

Thankfully all those worries dissipate the moment I hear her voice.

My sister is stronger than I give her credit for. It will take more than a loon with a biro to break our bond. She's proven the strength of the love between us time and time again throughout the years. I was a fool to even momentarily worry that something or someone so inconsequential could rip her from my life.

I exchange quick pleasantries with her and surprisingly she's the one who seems desperate to end the call rather than me, which has never happened before, and I feel mildly offended. She fobs me off with some bullshit about wanting to take a soak in the tub. I'm not sure what her real reasons are for needing me off the phone but I'm not about to waste real estate in my mind worrying about it. I trust May. There is no one on this earth I trust more to always have my best interests at heart. Perhaps she has a secret lover she's waiting for a call from?

The thought makes me laugh. Not the idea that my sister could have a lover. She's an attractive and successful woman. She should have a string of suitors knocking on her door. No, it's not the idea of May having a love affair that makes me laugh. It's the idea of her having a secret from me.

I can read her like a book, and anything she doesn't tell me willingly I have a sixth sense of sorts about. There is nothing I don't know about her. For example, I know that she's taken a leave of absence from her job and that she doesn't have a host of emails waiting for her response as she claims. I'll wait for her to tell me that though. No sense in confronting her with a secret so innocent.

My phone rings and I half expect it to be her, already riddled with guilt about her fibs to me. I'm pleasantly surprised however to see that it's James.

"James Coulson, how can I help?" I say.

"I'm downstairs in the lobby, but the receptionist has said you aren't taking meetings today?"

"Tell them I'll make an exception for you," I reply and he thanks me and then hangs up.

Quickly I catch sight of my reflection in the mirror I keep on my wall. It's a large brass monstrosity, but it belonged to my parents and May insisted I have it, so I can hardly sell it. There isn't a hair out of place on my head and thankfully my morning coffee hasn't stripped away my lipstick - I still look as put together as I did when Andrew picked me up. Perfect.

Once again I'm struck with the stupidity of my crush on Inspector Coulson. The last thing I need, with the party leadership up for grabs, is to be seen dating someone on the force.

For a start, it would open me up to questions about my impartiality, and if it all went wrong, then I would be the woman who mistreated one of the boys in blue, thus losing myself a large part of the union voters. No, there was no winning when it came to my feelings towards

James, but despite the dangers they'd bring to my career I couldn't deny them.

I've never been a woman to shy away from my feelings, no matter the trouble it brought to my door.

Even though I'm expecting him I still appreciate the way he knocks on my door and pauses, waiting for me to invite him in. He has manners and I find that very sexy in a man.

"Come in," I say, leaning back against my desk in a way that I know is flattering. It slims my waist and elongates my legs, it's the position I employ whenever I'm due to sit down with a member of the press. There's no harm in people finding you attractive. So long as they respect you as well.

"Isabella," he greets me, stepping forward with his hand outstretched. For a moment I watch his face as his eyes quickly scan my figure, and I don't look away when he finally makes eye contact. I want him to know that I've noticed him checking me out. That I appreciate it.

"Hi James," I say, standing straight and taking his hand. I shake it and then pull him towards me before kissing him on the cheek, taking in the scent of him. He smells clean and fresh, with no hint of cologne on his neck. I take a step back quickly, a way to let him know that the movement was nothing more than a greeting. I want him to work for it after all.

"I, um, yes." He's lost for words momentarily and it's adorable. The fact I can strip this powerful important man of sense with just the simplest of greetings thrills me. He wants me nearly as much as I want him. "Ahem. Yes. There's an update in your case."

I gesture towards the wingback armchairs in the corner of my office and we sit down in unison.

"We've checked the alibi of your ex-staffers and both can be accounted for whenever you have received a note or message. Their mobile phone data confirms the location they supplied in their statements." As he finishes speaking he looks towards me, concern and disappointment on his features.

He truly believed this case could be solved as easily as that. He'd hoped he could bring me news of my safety and instead, he has to let me know that once again he has no answers. That we have no answers. He thinks he's let me down.

"It's okay James," I lean forward and place my hand over his. "I know everyone is trying their best." I long to do more than just reassure him. I want to run my palm up his arm towards those tight shoulders and pull him towards me. To wrap my legs around his waist as I straddle him, feeling him swell against me. To run my tongue along his neck until he gasps my name. To feel his hands reach out and squeeze my breasts.

"Isabella?" James is staring at me and I realise I've allowed my focus to slip into a fantasy. I don't need to look into a mirror to know I'm blushing as I shift slightly in my chair, certain I can still feel him between my legs.

"Sorry, my mind was elsewhere. It's a busy day today," I try to explain.

"Oh of course, I'll leave you to it." He stands to leave.

"No. No, don't. That's not what I meant. Stay, stay. It's fine." I'm tripping over all over my words and I hope to God he finds it endearing because I'm finding it humiliating. Thankfully he flashes me a warm smile and I feel myself melt just a little further.

"It's fine, honestly. I have to be back at my desk soon anyway."

"If you're sure? I really don't mind if you want to hang around a bit longer?"

"I don't think the two of us spending time in your office 'hanging out' is going to achieve much, do you?" His tone is playfully scolding and I have to resist the urge to call him Sir.

Before this moment my attraction to James had simply been physical but with that sentence, he's made himself so much more interesting to me. There's a darker personality lurking behind his good looks and happy conversation, something more to him that needs exploring. Now I absolutely have to have him.

"Depends what the aim is I guess." I drop my voice slightly, leaving my lips slightly parted as I finish speaking, knowing it will draw his attention.

"Dinner. I'm going to take you out to dinner. As soon as this case is closed the two of us will spend some time really getting to know each other."

My knees feel weak as he makes this as a statement rather than a question. It feels so refreshing to have someone take the lead for once. If this man wants me, he can have me.

"Well then, you'd better get back to work," I say, turning my back on him and walking towards my desk chair, feeling his eyes on me as I do so. Sitting down and opening my laptop I make no further eye contact with him and the tension between us is thick.

I hear him laugh to himself as he turns on his heel and leaves my office. It takes all the self-control I have not to chase after him and drag him into the stairwell. Now I have even more of a reason to find the culprit behind the notes. Once the case is solved, James is going to take me on a real date, and I have a feeling it will be one I won't forget.

Then, like a cold bath on a winter's day, Andrew walks into my office and all the lust in my body evaporates.

"We've got a problem," he says, stating the obvious.

"If you hadn't been so quick to point the finger of blame then we wouldn't have."

"What? No. Not that. It's a problem with the votes." He replies, brushing off words that were meant to sting. I hate the way he's able to do that, to not care what others think of him, to switch off his emotions and get his head on straight. I can never work out if it irritates me so much because it repulses me or because I long to emulate it.

"The votes?" I ask, as though my brain isn't already racing ahead to the sentence that is coming next. I am behind in the polls. I do not have the support of my party.

"You're at least thirty votes behind the other candidate," he answers.

We have a rule that we do not speak the name of the man running against me for party leader, that we do not acknowledge his presence as anything more than an obstacle to overcome. He's only in the position he is now because he's riding the waves of his father's legacy. He himself has done nothing to deserve his name on the ballot, unlike me.

"What are their reasons?" I ask.

Andrew pushes a piece of paper towards me and with a slight quiver in my hand, I take it from him. I've come too far in life to lose this internal election. If I don't win this time, the first time, then the polish I've held around myself will dampen. I will no longer be the fast-rising wunderkind. I will be the woman who reached too far above her station and hit her head on the glass ceiling.

I scan my eyes over the short list of feedback points from my peers. The general consensus is that I'm not as likeable as my counterpart, I'm not as humane as him. I scoff, if they knew the reality behind the man they'd choose over me they'd change their views pretty quickly. At least I know the skeletons in my closet aren't locked under multiple NDAs for misconduct nobody dares speak about.

Momentarily I consider Andrew's suggestion from when we first began this race. The idea that a few leaked truths about my competitor's extracurricular preferences would be his downfall. At the time I'd dismissed this notion, convinced I had the support of my peers. That the good work I've done would speak for itself.

"I think it's time, don't you?" Andrew asks and I know he's referring to the photographs he has locked in his drawer. Photos of a man with a girl younger than his daughter. Photographs that will ruin so many lives.

"Let me think about it," I reply, knowing that Andrew won't be happy with this response, but at the end of the day, I'm the one who calls the shots. "I'll let you know in the morning."

With a sigh he plods out of my office, fingers already pulling his mobile phone from his pocket ready to fill my diary with meetings and appointments for the rest of the week. I wait until my door closes behind him before sinking into a chair. Tears form at the edges of my eyes but I'm too stubborn, too proud to let them fall. This can be fixed. One way or another I will be the leader of my party this year. I just had to reassess my tactics.

Chapter Ten - May

Isabella was home early from work today which suited me just fine. After snooping around her bedroom I'd felt so guilty that I'd busied myself cleaning and preparing a home-cooked meal for us both.

Her fridge was surprisingly well stocked. I'd assumed that with her always out entertaining that wouldn't be the case but I guess it's something else that Andrew takes care of for her. That's good of him. One less thing for her to worry about.

I'm trying to practice gratitude when it comes to Andrew and his presence in the shadows of my life. I'm never going to like the man but I should learn to tolerate him more. He does a good job looking out for my sister and that alone should buy him at least an ounce of my respect.

A lot of my feelings towards him are based on my own insecurities, as opposed to any failings on his part. I need to recognise that and adjust my attitude accordingly. I have to accept that he isn't going anywhere anytime soon, that he means a lot to Isabella and that at the moment he's the one best placed to help her achieve her dreams.

So when Isabella walks through the front door at 2 p.m. she's greeted by serenity. I'd even found a handful of candles in a cupboard and placed them around the place, hoping the scent of them might add some character.

Not that her house wasn't beautifully decorated, of course it was, and it was welcoming and comfortable. But there was something about it, something in the air that made the hairs on my arms bristle. Perhaps it's because I'd now seen the starkness of her bedroom, but whatever it was I wanted to ease its hold over her home.

I'm busy in the kitchen slowly cooking, too busy lost in the methodical bubbling of the pots and pans around me. Cooking has always helped centre me, it gives my mind something to focus on. Stirring a ragu sauce, I don't notice her come in. It's not until I hear her call out my name that I register her presence.

"May, this place looks amazing, you didn't have to do all of this," she says, gesturing around our spotless surroundings.

"Oh, it was nothing. Kept me busy is all." I reply, beaming inside at her compliment. I like to feel useful, always have. I guess acts of service are my love language - if you buy into that sort of thing.

"And God, that smells amazing but," she begins and my shoulders tense, preparing myself for her announcement that she already has plans for the night. That she hadn't been intending to spend time with me. "What I could do with right now though, is a glass of wine and a chat. Is that okay?"

I nod my head and turn off the hob, leaving a lid over the sauce to make sure it doesn't splatter all over what I just spent the last twenty minutes cleaning. Ragu always tastes better if you let it sit anyway. I was planning on making lasagne for dinner, a dish I know was Isabella's childhood favourite. Hopefully, she still enjoys it.

I watch as she collapses onto the sofa with a sigh, bottle of wine in one hand and two empty glasses held by their stems in the other.

If I'd attempted that movement the glasses would have hit each other and showered me in shards but she'd always been a precise person, every movement planned and executed to perfection. I can't remember her ever tripping up, though I'm sure it must have happened. Odds are it has anyway. She probably just styles it out so well that it looks intentional.

"What's up?" I ask, taking the bottle from her and cracking the screw top.

"It's the leadership contest," she replies, not making me fish for the truth like usual. For the first time in a long time, she's an open book. "I'm behind in the current polls."

"Oh Bella," I say, going to comfort her then quickly correcting myself. "Oh, Isabella, I'm so sorry. Can I do anything to help?"

I hope she says yes. I hope she gives me a task I can complete to aid her. To show her I can still be useful.

"I'm afraid not. Andrew has some ideas but I'm not sure about them, to be honest."

Of course Andrew has ideas. Andrew has everything.

I am grateful for Andrew. I am grateful for his presence in my sister's life.

I repeat this to myself over and over internally as I try to stop jealousy from seeping into my face. I fail though as Isabella squeezes my hand before taking the open bottle away from me.

She places both glasses on coasters on the table and pours us generous measures.

"To tell you the truth, what I could really do with is talking, about anything else. I just want to get my mind off it," she says, handing me a glass. I take a sip as I consider her request.

"Has Inspector Coulson gotten any further with those notes?"

"Jeez May. I meant something not quite so bleak. And no, James, hasn't found the perpetrator yet but he will." She laughs as she talks but I can see her bristle at my faux pas.

I should have known she wanted to speak about something mundane, something unrelated to her job. What she doesn't know though is that the question is all about self-preservation. If James doesn't know yet then that means Isabella doesn't know yet. Which means I still have time to come clean, The truth about the messages will be more palatable coming from me directly. I'll have a chance to explain before she flies off the handle.

"I was going to make lasagne for dinner, is that okay?" I ask instead of making any kind of confession.

"Mum's recipe?" Isabella asks as she pulls her hair out of the bun it's been tied in all day. I can almost hear the strands sigh with relief as they curl outwards finally able to enjoy their freedom.

"Of course. When you can make the best - " I begin.

"Why bother with the rest," she finishes and we both let out a small snuff of a laugh. Mum used to say that every time we went out for dinner and one of us considered ordering lasagne. Sometimes, even now, when I go out to eat I order one just so I can imagine her false annoyed expression when it arrives.

Sinking back into the plump cushions of the sofa I feel myself relax, and I know that Isabella feels the same. It's like she's left the rest of the world at the front door and right now she's just my sister. Just my Bella.

"So," I start, ready to broach an unusual topic of conversation for us, "how are things with Inspector, I mean James?"

It's not that me and my sister don't talk every day. We genuinely do, every evening we call each other whilst preparing our evening meals. It's just our topics of conversation stick exclusively to work or the latest television show. I'm rarely allowed to delve into her personal life, especially not her romantic personal life. Not since Marcus.

No matter what Isabella says, I know that she loved that man. She truly did. Which was a shame as he was a cad of extreme proportions, in fact, and I don't tend to swear too often, he was a complete and utter arsehole. One of those types that fell from the Narcissus family tree. There was never a doubt in my mind that Marcus would drown staring at his reflection.

Once he left her life though, so did all traces of real conversations with my sister. It was my fault really. I kept pushing her to tell me how she really felt when he up and left. I went on and on at her, until eventually she shut me out. Even now I want to ask her how she feels about him now he's passed away, whether she has any regrets or grief towards the man she once loved. I don't though. I can't risk her putting any more distance between us.

For a moment she stares at me, as though she can't quite believe I've dared to ask her such a personal question. As though I'm nothing more than a prying journalist overstepping my mark in some interview or another. Then she takes a sip of wine and her face softens. In a flash, she switches from politician back to my sister.

"I like him," momentarily shocked by her own admission. "Probably more than I should."

"Why shouldn't you like him?"

"Well, he's in the force. It can only end badly."

I consider her worries for a moment, mostly because they don't make any sense to me. Surely a politician and a police officer make for a wonderful PR story? Especially if it ends up in a happily ever after.

"I'm sorry, I don't understand what you mean. Why would it end badly? Is he married or something?"

She looks hurt by my question, and I feel ashamed. Of course my sister would never get involved with a man that was already spoken for. We were raised better than that. I made sure she was raised better than that.

"It's okay May, I don't expect you to understand."

She leans forward and generously refills her glass and I breathe a sigh of relief. It seems she isn't completely averse to having a personal conversation this evening. If she were, my question about James would have led to her excusing herself to 'freshen up' for dinner.

I follow suit and top up my glass, though it's not nearly as empty as hers. I hold the bottle in my hand and stare at the label. I remember this wine. This used to be Mum's favourite brand. I can't believe Isabella drinks it. Or maybe she doesn't remember.

Her eyes are on me, I can tell because my skin is prickling. It always did when I was the sole focus of my sister's gaze. She could be such an intense person. She didn't mean anything by it, she's always been that way, always been intrigued with people watching.

"Do you remember," I begin.

"It was mum's favourite," she finishes, staring into her glass wistfully.

"Why do we never talk about them?" I ask, and it's a question I've held my tongue on so many times since the night they passed away.

"What do you want to talk about? How much they're missed? How tragic it was?"

"No. No. Nothing like that. Just about them in general. They were our parents after all."

She considers my point, I can see her thought process as she ruminates on my request.

"Do you remember the last time we ate together as a family?" Isabella asks me with a lazy smile on her face. And of course I do.

"Mum made lasagne and had a few too many glasses of wine," I say with a laugh.

"Dad was pretending to be annoyed at her but really he was just jealous."

"Oh yeah, because he had to be the designated driver."

Now it's Isabella's turn to chuckle. I do find it slightly jarring that the first memory of our parents she's ever wanted to talk about is the meal we had right before we lost them, but beggars can't be choosers. "Who were they going out with again?"

"Roy and his wife," I reply. Roy was Dad's business partner. The four of them often socialised but that night was going to be different. They were celebrating a potential acquisition and Dad had spent all evening pacing the hallway in excitement before Mum finally calmed him down enough to eat.

"Oh yeah, they came to the house before they all left together didn't they?" she remembers.

Sometimes I forget that Isabella is younger than me, given she's the dominant personality in our relationship. She might not have as sharp a memory of that night as I do. Roy, his wife, mum and dad had all sat in the kitchen sharing a drink before heading off to their dinner reservations.

Reservations they never arrived to because Dad crashed the car off the side of a cliff. They were all dead on arrival according to the paramedic's report.

Occasionally I wonder if Dad had perhaps had a sneaky drink or two before they set off. It would explain why he didn't brake in time for the curve in the road. Too confident in his own driving ability, it was a road he drove multiple times a day. That wasn't like my father though. If he said he was going to stay sober, he would have. He had his faults sure, but he always kept his word.

"You really don't remember?" I ask.

"Some days I find it harder than others. But I never know if it's because I don't have the memories, or if it's because I've forgotten them." She replies with a level of honesty that stirs something in the recesses of my mind. I know what it's like to lock memories away, to force yourself to forget them, or at least I feel like I do.

If I try too hard to think back to difficult periods in my life they get a little hazy, and disjointed in their playback - like a video that's streaming but not fully loaded. My past is constantly buffering. I'm about to explain to my sister that I know how she feels when I sense a shift in her demeanour.

Her smile begins to fade and her jaw tightens, her grip on the wine glass in her hand tightens and I know that the walls have come back up. My breathing feels shallow, and I try to take a deep breath but it doesn't reach my lungs. So I take another. And then another. But it's still not enough. There isn't enough oxygen in my body. I'm going to die if I can't take a real breath soon. My head feels dizzy and then, all of a sudden, a sense of rage descends upon me.

How dare Isabella just decide we were done for the evening. She doesn't get to call all the shots. She shouldn't be the one calling all the shots. She never makes good decisions and I always have to deal with the fallout from them. She's a selfish and dangerous creature and she needs to be contained.

I look her in the eyes and my blood begins to boil, I hate this woman.

I hate her.

I haven't felt this angry since the night I lost Chris. Since the night he left.

I hate my sister.

I hate her for all the decisions she's ever made under the guise of looking out for me.

I hate her.

"May?" she asks, as she scooches away from me on the sofa.

Then, as though it never happened, the blinding anger leaves my system. It was irrational. I don't know where it stemmed from and I hate the way my baby sister is looking at me now. She saw the madness in my eyes, I know she did. She couldn't have missed it. She'd have to be blind to have missed the hatred emanating from me out towards her.

"May?" she asks again and I stand from the sofa.

"I'm sorry. I should get dinner started." I say, taking a step towards the kitchen.

"Are you still taking your medication?" she asks and I bristle at her curiosity. "It helped you a lot after mum and dad."

"I know," I reply, my tone sharper than I intended. "I know, yes, I still take it, every day just like Dr. Jones recommended."

"Good. And you know I'm here if you ever need me?"

"Yes Bella, I know." I turn around and shoot her a smile, wanting her to know that everything is okay between us as I leave the living room and return to the kitchen.

Chapter Eleven - Isabelle

May had worried me earlier.

So worried that I haven't been able to sleep yet. I'm lying in my bed, wide awake trying not to stare at my clock. I'm trying desperately not to walk too far down memory lane but it's hard. Every time I close my eyes I remember that look on her face when I tried to end the conversation about our parents.

It wasn't so much that I didn't enjoy talking about mum and dad, nor is it because I miss them. Our relationship had broken down to just the essentials years before they died. But it wasn't good for May to wallow in the past. There were things from that time period it's better she doesn't think about, for both our sakes.

She'd looked at me with such hatred on her features that for a brief moment I thought I was going to have to take action. Thankfully the moment passed and she brought herself back in line. But it had happened. And that means that maybe my big sister is no longer as trustworthy as I'd thought she was. She claims she's still taking her medication, I'll have to check her pill bottle in the morning just to be sure.

I can't have her breaking down like she did after we lost our parents. The scene she'd caused at their funeral had been the talk of the town for months. And the way she'd lunged at me at the wake - well, let's just say nobody had questioned the decision to section her for a week.

After a brief stint in the Sanctuary she'd come home as nearly the same person I'd known growing up. Quieter though, more careful with her thoughts and feelings. I guess that's to be expected though when you feel you can't trust your own mind.

And the way she's been after Chris.

No.

I can't think about that too much. The state she'd been in. The things I had to do to help her.

And so that's why I'm lying here awake at 2 a.m. Because for the first time in a long time I'm not in control of what the immediate future will bring. And that chills me to the bone. I've worked so hard for everything I have, but now all my plans are on shaky ground. My feet are no longer on the steady path I'd painstakingly laid for myself many, many years ago.

If I'm being honest though, worrying about May isn't the only thing keeping my mind from settling. At the moment, time in bed is the only time I get to be truly alone.

Despite my career and the socialising it carries with it, I'm a solitary creature. I'm very much used to my home being my safe space. The one place where I don't need to wear a mask.

But with my sister living here that isn't possible anymore. I still have to keep my switches on when in her presence. I can't just zone out and be myself. I know she'd worry if she saw that side of me. The detached side. The side that likes to simply run through the motions without any feeling whatsoever.

I take no pleasure in food, it's merely fuel to keep my body working. But with May here every meal is a show. I have to be sure to really taste the flavours on my plate so I can interact with her accordingly.

There is no joy for me in any form of entertainment, and trust me, I've tried it all. Television shows, movies, music, books, video games, board games and God forbid even podcasts - none of it holds my interest for longer than ten seconds. It's all just so, pointless.

There is only one thing that matters in my life, and that's my career. That's the only thing I feel truly passionate about, instead of the shiny version of interest I paint on for the surrounding world.

Did I watch the latest episode of the show everyone is talking about? Christ no. But did I read the synopsis enough to join in with conversations about it? Of course. I need to keep up appearances when I am outside this house. I have to appear normal - like everybody else.

When someone asks me about my interests, I would love to tell them that I have none.

That when I eventually get home from a day at work I merely sit in my living room and stare at the wall until it's an acceptable time to go to bed. I can sit completely still like that for hours, I have done it countless nights. Most in fact. It's how I'd prefer to spend most of my life. It's almost like meditation, but I don't know peace. I don't know joy. I don't know sorrow, I just know silence and that suits me.

If May knew that she would be beside herself. She'd be so certain that something was wrong with me. My sister feels so much. Too much. It's why she's the way she is. She would try to fix me, which would be insulting because I'm not broken. I'm just; different.

So sharing my private space like this is exhausting. Having to constantly play a part, it's nearly more than I can handle.

Nearly.

So I need to sort out this mystery with the messages and get my sister back into her own life. For both our sakes. If the state she got herself into earlier is anything to go by, then being around me this much isn't healthy for her either. It's bringing up bad memories, whether she's aware of it or not. And I can't have that. May can't become a loose cannon again. There's too much at risk.

It's now 3 a.m. and I have a full day of meetings ahead of me. I need a plan. Once I have a plan I'll be able to switch off and rest. It has to be a good one though, one nobody will see through. If May knows of my concern for her there's a chance she'll tiptoe closer to the edge I can't let her fall from.

Andrew won't be happy with my plan though. He has it in for May and has told me as much. It's basically an item on our daily to-do list - what to do about the 'May problem' as he calls it.

So far, I've managed to ignore his consistent pleas that she's a danger, but I don't know how much longer I can turn a blind eye. I love my sister, I do, and I'd do anything to keep her safe. So Andrew is just going to have to go along with my plan and keep all his paranoid asides to himself.

Perhaps I need to have a quiet conversation with him and remind him who's actually in the driving seat. Why can't he be more like Agatha, my old assistant. She never asked uncomfortable questions, or made me justify my decisions. She was just proud of me, supportive of me, everything that Andrew no longer is.

He's growing far too big for his breeches, making decisions that he'd usually defer to me on and if I don't bring him back in line then I'll have to consider letting him go.

It would be a shame though. The man is loyal to a fault, he's been by my side since we met at university and has played a key part behind the scenes in all my success to date. I'd hate to carry on along this journey without him but if he steps too far out of line, if he thinks he can start giving me orders, I'll be left with no choice. I make the decisions in my life. Always have, always will.

Yes. I'll take May into the office with me tomorrow. Tell her that there's some kind of admin emergency I need her help with. She'll like that. It will appeal to her ego. May has always liked to feel indispensable, as though she's the only one who can save the day. That's probably why she and Andrew hate each other so much.

They think I don't see it but I do. They believe that they hide their resentment well when I'm in the room. But it's there behind every word they utter towards each other, the stolen glances when they think my attention is elsewhere. I can't believe I ever set the two of them up on a date! What was I thinking?

Well, I know what I was thinking. I was looking for something to make May happy. She'd been so broken after the Chris thing ended that I wanted to show her there were plenty more fish in the sea. And if one of those fish just so happened to be my campaign manager then so be it. On paper, they were a great match. They shared so many interests that conversation should have flowed easily between them all night.

But it was hate at first sight between them. Both competing to be the alpha dog in my life. Pathetic really. If they'd just seen the bigger picture maybe they could have put their jealousies aside and enjoyed a nice meal together.

The two of them are not as clever as they think they are - if they were they'd have figured out it's better to be allies than enemies if they hoped to keep me in line. Sorry, to keep me safe, as they like to call it.

If May is in the office tomorrow at least I can keep an eye on her. I can make sure she doesn't do anything stupid.

I'm pretty sure she's been snooping around my room whilst I've been gone. And I can't have that. There's no concrete evidence for my suspicions though, everything is exactly as I left it down to the tightness my comforter is tucked in by, but it's a feeling I have. Like somebody's been poking around inside my brain.

Once I concluded that she'd been in my room, there was a part of me that wanted to march into her room and confront her. In the way I would have done when we were growing up and she'd 'borrowed' some item of clothing or another.

God, we used to have such screaming matches over the most trivial things. Maybe I'll remind her of that in the morning, we could reminisce and joke about past arguments to have us avoid a present day one. She'd like that. Yes. I'll make sure to bring that up on the car ride to the office.

Turning onto my side I pull the duvet up to my chin. Now I can finally concentrate on falling asleep. Tomorrow I will take May with me to work. Perhaps I'll speak to James about keeping an eye on her over the next few days so I can at least get some work done. There are a few loose ends that need to be tied up before the party election is officially underway.

James.

Inspector Coulson.

Now there's a much more enjoyable train of thought to keep me awake. Closing my eyes now I picture him…

Standing in my office, gazing at me with hungry eyes. He can't have me though, not yet, he has to work for it first. But before I can tell him that he marches across the floor towards me until our faces are millimetres from each other. He's going to kiss me, I know. This is always my favourite moment, the one right before the first kiss. The sexual tension between us is electric and I can't help but lean forward first. My lips brush against his softly and I reach my hands up towards his face, wanting to pull him closer to me.

He grabs hold of my wrists and pulls back, shaking his head at me, a serious expression knitted onto his face. Have I misread his signals? Over-egged his interest in me? Embarrassment growls in my stomach. I never let a man have the upper hand, not anymore, not since Marcus -

No -

I'm not going to think about Marcus right now. I'm going to lie here and indulge in fantasies about the Inspector as I finally unwind for the evening. My hand traces the movements he's making in my imagination as the meaning behind his serious expression becomes clear.

Using his knee he gently parts my legs, removing his hands from my wrists he places them on my thighs. Inching his way closer and closer to the place where I need him most.

With a happy sigh, I lean towards my bedside cabinet and open the bottom drawer. Yes, I'm going to be exhausted in the morning, but at least I'll be drinking my coffee with a smile on my face.

Chapter Twelve - May

I know I'm only being invited into the inner sanctum of her office so Isabella can keep an eye on me. Ever since I lost control of my emotions last night, she's kept one eye on me at all times.

I don't know why I felt so angry at her. I've thought about the moments preluding it over and over. It's not like Isabella hasn't shut down conversation with me before, I'm used to it by now. It's usually water off a duck's back but something about last night, something in our conversation stirred feelings in me that I'd rather keep under wraps. Nothing good can come from poking around in your subconscious too much.

So now, I'm sitting on the floor of one of Isabella's offices, boxes of paperwork surrounding me, pretending to find Andrew's filing system fantastically creative as opposed to absolutely incorrect. Who doesn't file in subcategories? Or at least alphabetically?

What kind of maniac just shoves everything in according to their own system?

The kind of maniac who wants to make themselves indispensable that's who. Thankfully the before-mentioned lunatic has finally left me alone. After listening to a half-hour lecture about his preferences for storing information, I'm ready to go home, but it's only just coming up to lunchtime so I know there's no chance of that.

Now that I'm sure Isabella has worked out I'm on annual leave she's determined to keep me busy and underfoot. I really can't hide anything from my sister, she must have read the lie in my expression when I told her I had e-mails to answer. She knows me better than I know myself.

The box I'm currently working my way through has information on each of Isabella's donors and supporters. An endless reel of cookie-cutter people. All of whom line up at every benefit to keep my sister in her position, and who hope she'll help them further up the ladder when she succeeds. They know as well as I do that it's a case of when she ascends to the next rung rather than if. It's impossible to meet my sister and not share in her self-belief.

Satisfied I've reached the end of my current pile of paperwork, I push the empty box away from me and pull the next one into its position with a sigh. Today is going to be one of those days that never ends. You get a lot of days like that as an accountant, so it's not that I'm afraid of repetitive tasks, it's just I'd rather do anything else but them.

I could just tell Isabella I'm going to cut my annual leave short and head home. Nothing is stopping me from boarding a train tonight and making my way back to my own flat. My own bed. My own mind-numbing tasks.

She'd argue against me of course. Tell me she was keeping me safe by keeping me close, but I knew that there was no danger. There was no stranger out there with a poison pen. It was just me, myself and I. And if she knew that she'd probably pack my bags herself.

Hopefully, it wouldn't come to that but I can't stay living with her for much longer. I've outstayed my welcome, that much is obvious from Isabella's fraying nerves - she thinks she hides them so well but I know her well too. I can see parts of her she'd rather keep hidden.

I need my own space. That's probably why I lost control of my temper the other night. I'm feeling caged in. I thought this was what I wanted. To be back in my sister's life in a leading role, but it turns out I much preferred being a support player in the Isabella show. It's too much living life her way every day.

I'll speak to her about it tonight. I'll be kinder than that but I need to go home. This plan has run its course and backfired spectacularly. It's time to go home.

It's time to go home.

It's time to go home.

I catch myself muttering those five words like I'm bloody Dorothy in Oz and shake my head. Onto the next box of paperwork. I just need to get through these tasks and then tonight I'll settle into a seat on the train and watch this world slip away from me. Perfect.

Because I'm so busy daydreaming about leaving Isabella behind I almost miss the photograph tucked inside the folder.

A photograph of Samantha and Isabella, of their teenage selves.

A moment of friendship is captured on film. The two of them have their heads pushed close together as they whisper something amongst themselves. I can remember them like that. They were so codependent. Two halves of the same whole. Spending all day every day together until suddenly; they weren't. Until Samantha was a name we never spoke in my house.

As though she'd never existed. As though the friendship between the two of them hadn't consumed everything individual about them. When they were together there was no Samantha and Isabella, there was just them. The girls.

Gravity doesn't work like that! You did that! You!

Beast. She's a beast. Never again. You will never see that girl again.

I can hear the remnants of a conversation I stole from my parents and Isabella. I sat at the top of the stairs, peering through the bannisters as the three of them argued in the kitchen. Mum and Dad in their best clothes, ready for a night of celebrations for their anniversary, screaming in my sister's face.

Staring at the photo before me, I try to bring more of that memory back to me, but once again my memories are stuck on pause and this time, for the first time, I want them to play. I want to know what it is that I've worked so hard to forget. It's no use though, you can't undo years of conditioning in just a minute.

I open the folder the photo slipped from and find inside a mini-biography of Samantha. But of adult Samantha. It lists her place of residence, and current occupation (none) and even contains details of her multiple stints in local rehabilitation facilities. Just as I'm about to get lost in the folders pages a deep cough comes from the doorway.

Throwing the folder to the floor as though it's scalded me, I look up to find Andrew watching me curiously. Without speaking a word he steps towards me, lifts the folder from my hands and closes it.

"I have background files on everybody who's ever been important in your sister's life," he offers by way of an explanation as he turns to leave.
"Yours is perhaps the largest," he adds as the door closes behind him.

I watch him go, taking with him the questions I should have asked whilst I had the chance.

Why was Samantha still considered a person of interest? If he had a file on me did that mean he also had one on Marcus? Was Andrew really only protecting Isabella's career trajectory, or did he have a different reason for digging out all this information about people who'd passed through her orbit?

I've always wondered if he were perhaps a little bit in love with my sister. Now I'm almost certain that he is.

There's no way Isabella would have agreed to him running these, frankly illegal, background checks on such insignificant players in her life.

How did he get his hands on Samantha's medical records? Has he managed to get a hold of mine? My skin prickles at the thought of his eyes running themselves over the most private parts of my life.

No.

Andrew has no right to poke around in my past. In anyone's.

I need to speak to Isabella. She needs to know what he's up to.

But I need to be careful. If he's truly as obsessed with her as I now believe him to be, that means he's not someone to be trifled with. He's made it clear time and time again that he'll go to many lengths to protect my sister, and I need to make sure that he doesn't view me as a threat. I don't know what he's capable of.
Or do I?

Samantha has only just been found dead. What if Andrew decided to neutralise something he viewed as an obstacle for Isabella? Could he have taken it that far?

No.

I'm letting paranoia creep in. That's always been my problem, my brain isn't wired right. It hasn't been since the night we lost our parents.

I have an overactive imagination and I need to stop. Murderers are rare and Andrew is not one.

Samantha died of a drug overdose, sad but true.

I've seen the evidence of her addiction in her medical records. I scanned the long list of clinics and councillors she'd used to try and free herself of her demons. And clearly, it just wasn't enough.

If, and it's a big if, Andrew had somehow been responsible for her death he would be stupid to leave his dossier on her around for anyone to find. And Andrew is not a stupid man.

The next few hours go by in a flash as I work on autopilot until all the paperwork boxes are emptied and flattened, stacked up neatly against the wall, ready for recycling. I'm about to pop out of the office and ask someone where they need to be disposed of when Isabella sticks her head around the door frame.

"I'm going to clock off early, do you want a lift home?"

Home. Her use of that word sparks happiness in me. She didn't describe the place as hers, she didn't ask me if I wanted a lift back to hers, she said home. As in our home.

That's going to make what I have to do harder.

Because I'm still resolved to tell her that I'm leaving tonight. My earlier thoughts about Andrew are just evidence that I need to get back to my home, my real home, and get back into the routine that keeps me stable sooner rather than later.

All this drama, admittedly of my creation, isn't doing anything good for my mental health.

If I stay there's no guarantee that I won't fall off the deep end again and require medical intervention. And I don't want that. I don't know if my life can recover from that again.

As we make our way down to the lobby I can't shake the feeling that somebody's watching me. I glance back up the stairs we've walked down and sure enough there's Andrew. Watching me like a hawk watches its prey. Arms flung casually over the railing at the top, manilla folder dangling from his fingers. He notices me watching and taps two fingers against the file before walking away.

I can't leave my sister.

I can't.

What if I'm not going mad?

What if Andrew did kill Sam?

Isabella isn't safe with him, not if he's that obsessed with her. Sooner or later he'll confess his feelings and I don't know how he'll react if, or rather when, she rejects him.

I need to find evidence of what he's done and take it to the police, to Inspector Coulson. Then I can go back home.

I have to put Isabella first right now, she's my sister and I can't let anything bad happen to her. Not when I can do something to stop it.

We're driven home by Isabella's regular driver. Or at least I assume he is, given the conversation they exchange on the journey. She asks after his family, how his eldest is getting on at university - all the right questions with all the appropriate responses in turn. I really do envy her ability to do that.

I get tongue-tied at the slightest hint of small talk. My words have a habit of running away with themselves and then I lie awake in bed replaying every interaction until I've convinced myself that I'd acted like a social failure.

Granted, it's never as bad as I imagine but the mental ramifications of forced socialisation just aren't worth it to me anymore.

It's strange though because when I was young I used to be the life and soul of every party. I was 'that' girl at school - the one who knew everyone's name and signed everyone's yearbook. That girl died though the same night Mum and Dad did. That girl had to grow up overnight and keep what was left of her family together, no matter the costs to herself.

Before I know it we're outside Isabella's house and she's holding the door open for me. In unison we both put our shoes away, hang our coats and she leaves her briefcase by the front door.

"How was your day?" Isabella asks me as she moves towards the kitchen.

"It was okay," I begin, "well actually, there was something kind of strange."

"Oh God, yes I know. Andrew's filing system is the worst, isn't it? I can never find anything I'm looking for but whenever I ask him for anything, bam, there it is. So I guess it works for him." She's laughing lightly at Andrew's strange little foible as she rummages through the fridge. She selects two steaks and a bag of salad.

"No, it's not that," I interject.

She's busy pulling out pans and various spices so I know she isn't really listening to me.

"Is steak okay for dinner?" she asks as she opens the packet and clicks the hob on. It's a question I am not supposed to have anything but a positive answer to and so I nod.

"I found something, in one of the files." I start.

"Mmhmm" she replies, dashing a little oil into the pan with one hand, as she lifts the steaks from their plastic tray with another. I don't know how she has the stomach to touch raw meat like that, so carelessly, I always have to use a spatula.

"Isabella, can you please just stop for a second and listen to me?" I ask my own rhetorical question. Surprisingly she obeys with no pushback, even going so far as to turn the hob off.

"Andrew had a file of information on Samantha." I wait for her reaction, but her eyebrow barely twitches in surprise.

"He has files on everyone in my life. We put them together when I won my seat. A way to make sure everything was documented should somebody, as Marcus did, try to sell a story on me." Her explanation was plausible but it didn't explain why Andrew's information was so up to date.

"It wasn't just that though, everything in there was current, like about who she was now rather than who she was then. He even had her medical records!" I nearly shout the last part at her, wanting to press on her the importance of what I'd stumbled upon.

This bit of information does appear to have shocked her somewhat and she takes a deep breath in through her nose before replying.

"Well, he certainly shouldn't have that. I'll speak to him about it tomorrow."

"Bella, he said he has a file on me?"

"Of course he doesn't. You're my sister, I know you'd never do anything to hurt me."

I can feel my cheeks flush warm as I remember sending her that first message.

I know what you did.

The message that started all of this. She's right, normally I would never do anything to hurt her, but when I sent that message I wasn't normal. I wasn't right in the head.

"No, of course I wouldn't," I say, not sure if I'm lying or not. Sometimes it's like there are two versions of me, co-existing in one brain. One that would never, ever want to hurt her sister. And a smaller one. A much, much smaller one, that wants to break her.

Christ. That's the first time I've ever admitted that to myself in such vulgar, raw terms. It's what caused me to get so angry the other night. There's a tiny part of me, a minuscule one that wants to punish Isabella for acts I can't even recall. See I told you, I'm not wired right.

"Right, so I'll speak to Andrew in the morning and see what he has to say for himself. Now, shall I carry on with dinner?"

I'm so caught up in my thoughts that all I can do is nod. I can't get my head around the fact that even a sliver of me hates my little sister. It's not right. I've given up everything to protect her.

As I walk upstairs to my room to change into my jogging bottoms I do find myself wondering if that part of me exists because of what I've had to give up.

Because of who.

Chapter Thirteen - Isabella

May went to bed just after dinner, and I took the opportunity to call Andrew and invite him over for a drink.

So now I find myself sitting at the bottom of my garden, hidden from view as I wait for him to arrive. It's not that I'm trying to hide his presence from my sister, it's just better for her if she doesn't know he's here.

"You rang?" he asked, his voice appearing from the shadows as he did his best Lurch impression. Usually, this would at least draw a smile from me, after all, I'd enjoyed watching The Addams Family growing up, but I was too preoccupied to play pretend right now.

"I think you might be right about May," I say.

"I've told you all along that you couldn't trust her," he replies in a condescending tone.

"You need to remember your place Andrew," I say, making sure each of my words are clipped with a warning.

His ego is getting the better of him these days and I can't have that. He's running the risk of stepping out of line. Sometimes he forgets that despite our close working relationship that it is just that. A working relationship.

One in which I am the employer and he the employee. Once again I'm struck with a longing for simpler times, when Agatha was still with us she was the ying to his yang. Always waiting, knitting in hand, with a kind word to calm me when he'd pushed one of my buttons. Maybe I let the wrong person go that day.

"Sorry," he says, looking anything but. I know he isn't a fan of when I pull rank, but sometimes it has to be done.

"You're wrong about her though. I can trust her. There's no one I trust more than my sister."

He looks wounded by words, and if I were a more empathetic person I'd care. I don't have time for his petty jealousy or to pander to his feelings. We have work to do.

"Of course," he replies, relying on his sycophantic nature to keep his emotions in check.

"I'm going to ask James to keep an eye on her. Make sure she doesn't put herself in any danger."

"You should send her away." He's been asking this of me since the day she arrived; trying to convince me that sending her back for a stint in the Sanctuary is the answer to all my problems. It isn't though. I'm not ready to make that decision yet. I still have hope that she'll sort herself out and that some deep-seated part of her brain will realise some things are better left forgotten.

"That isn't an option. Now, tell me what's going on in the press?"

He pulls out his phone and with a few swipes of his fingers opens a story from a small newspaper located up North. It's a story about Samantha and her death, the journalist whose name resides in the byline thinks there's more to it than a simple overdose.

They knew Samantha personally as a member of their local recovery group and were adamant that she was clean. I'm sure she was, but addicts are always in danger of falling off the wagon again. None more so than the girl I once knew.

Samantha had introduced me to smoking, drinking and boys.

Before we became friends, I'd been a naive little weirdo, always on the outskirts of social functions. But for the year she was by my side, I was one-half of the friendship people wanted to be a part of.

People knew our names. We dominated every classroom we walked into simply by existing. There wasn't a party or homework club we weren't invited to, not that we went to them all, we were much too aloof for that.

I guess that was part of our appeal to others. We didn't want their adoration and so they gave it to us willingly. She was always the leader though, the one who dreamt up the pranks or forged the letters to get us out of PE. I'd never had a friend like her and I haven't had one since.

She introduced me to the spotlight, taught me how to keep people in line simply with words, and showed me that there was more to life than trying to win my parent's approval. The year we spent together forever changed me. It altered my DNA and gave my life purpose and drive. I'd truly loved her.

But then.

Then Kayla appeared on the scene.

Kayla with her perfect hair and melodic laugh.

Kayla who knew where we could get served without ID.

Kayla who could manipulate grown men with just a smile.

At first, I'd thought she was just a passing fancy. That Samantha would tire of her presence and we would go back to being the gruesome twosome as Dad called us. But when she invited Kayla to the old pier with us that night I knew she was destined to be a permanent fixture in my life.

The pier was our secret place, somewhere we'd never invited anyone else to. We knew every nook and cranny and had shared many secrets within its rotten walls.

So for her to invite Kayla there with us, that was a big deal. We were only eleven, but I knew that night that Samantha had made a decision that would alter both of our lives forever. I didn't want to be friends with Kayla, and after Samantha had invited her to join us, I didn't particularly want to be friends with Samantha anymore either. If she couldn't see that we worked better as a pair than as a trio then she wasn't worth keeping in my life.

Which is why, later that week, when my parents were shouting and screaming at me about that night on the pier it barely hurt when they said I could never see Samantha again. I'd already let go of our friendship anyway. So no, all these years later I hadn't been surprised to learn of Samantha's overdose. The careless and impulsive girl had grown into the exact type of woman I knew she would.

"And why does this matter?" I ask Andrew, pushing the phone away from me back towards his chest. He was wasting my time and with each view of the story, lining the pockets of the two-buck journalist behind it.

"They think Samantha was linked to Marcus," and now the reason for his interest in this article is clear.

"How?" it's implausible that two large parts of my past could have interlinked without me knowing. If she'd met Marcus when I was dating him then my name would have come up in conversation between them. I'd bet half my net worth that he still name-dropped me wherever possible in the years since we broke up. Well, since he left me.

There was still a shadow of a sting when I look back on that period in my life. I wouldn't say I regret the day he walked out of my life, nor any of the days that followed, but it's certainly a time period I don't enjoy dwelling in. I let him get too close, and finally believed I found someone who could love me despite my oddities. But all he'd seen was a meal ticket in a pretty dress, that much was clear when he moved out of my house - making sure to take my credit cards with him.

I never did press charges against him. I wanted to appear to be the bigger person. To let him think he'd gotten one over on me. So no, despite May's questions I don't feel even a glimmer of grief over his murder. That man got what was coming to him.

"Back when Samantha used to hold down a job she worked at a local dive bar. Marcus used to use it to meet certain clientele." Andrew replies, disdain dripping from the last word to leave his lips.

He'd seen first-hand how broken I'd been after Marcus had left. He helped pick up the pieces, and it was comforting to see he still hated the man even in death. Andrew is a loyal person, perhaps I should be softer with him now and again.

"And what, pray tell, has the journalist deduced from this?" I pull my coat tighter around myself and glance up towards my house. May's room is still in darkness - good. The last thing I need is for her to glance out of the window and spot us - lord knows what conclusions her paranoid mind would jump to.

"They seem to think the deaths are somehow related. Maybe Marcus made a deal in the bar that went south and Samantha was a loose end that needed tying up."

"Hm, I suppose that does seem plausible."

"It won't be long until this story spreads, and once they publicly link Samantha to Marcus, and Marcus back to you they'll come sniffing around for a statement."

"And they'll try to drag my name through the mud too."

"Exactly. They'll twist the whole thing and make out like you keep the company of low-rent gangsters and drug-addled wrecks."
It's inspiring to see how much Andrew cares about me and my reputation. Although, my success is his success as he always says.

"Let's get ahead of it then. Draft a statement and we'll release it in the morning. If we're the first to make the link then we control the angle."

He nods at me and slides his phone back into his pocket.

"And May?" He asks.

Damn it Andrew, just as I was starting to see your positives again you have to circle back to the point that's driving such a wedge between us.

"May is none of your concern. She's my sister and she will be fine." I speak with the conviction that my heart is lacking. Will she be fine? Can I keep her fine?

"As you wish," he nods at me and then turns and disappears through the hedges at the back of my garden. His obsession with my sister is beginning to become an inconvenience.

I need his head in the game. Especially at the moment whilst I'm polling down against my competitor. The last thing I need is for some sloppy mistake to tarnish my reputation. That really would put the nail in the coffin of my leadership run.

I have to win the first time I run. I have to. If I lose then I'll always be the runner-up, no matter how much success comes after it. I'll always be the second choice and I can't have that. I can't be someone's second choice again. I have to win.

Shaking my head to myself I pick my way back up my garden path towards my home. Taking care to lock the back door behind me I pause at my fridge. There's still at least a glass of wine left in the bottle we opened with dinner.

It could help take the edge off my conversation with Andrew.

Why couldn't he just let the May thing go?

I've looked after her for so many years, protected her - I know what's best for her and he needs to understand that. The last thing I need is somebody whispering in my ear, reminding me there's an easier solution than helping her.

No.

Wine isn't the answer right now.

Bed is.

So I turn off the lights downstairs and make my way to my bedroom; its starkness instantly bringing calm to my spirit. If I could control the rest of the world the way I can control this room then I'd be at peace. In here there's no clutter, nothing to distract my mind when it needs to think. There is just me and shelter. Exactly the way I like it.

Chapter Fourteen - May

I realised last night, as I lay in bed with just my resentment for company, that it didn't matter if there was a part of me that hated my sister. Surely that's just part of being a sibling?

I did try to search online about it, and granted most of the results I found pointed me in the direction that these feelings weren't quite standard in healthy relationships. But I did find one of two examples that I could relate to. That helped me feel a little better. As my therapist used to tell me, we have to understand our feelings in order to confront them.

Granted, I wasn't ready yet to do the real work at digging into the root of these feelings, but I had acknowledged them so that was a start. There'd be time to sort all of that out later. For now, I had to work out if my suspicions were correct about Andrew.

I didn't buy the excuse that he had Samantha's medical records under the guise of looking out for one of Isabella's friends.

If that were the case he would have told my sister. She would have stepped in to offer Samantha care at a top facility, I know she would have. But she had no idea that her drug use had gotten such a grip on the poor woman. So no, Andrew's explanation of events hadn't satisfied my curiosity. It had only fanned the flames.

She'd tried to invite me into the office with her again today, but I'd made up an excuse about having a headache. Eventually, she'd bought it, but I could tell she was reluctant to leave me by myself. She thinks I'm losing my mind again. She hasn't said as much but I can tell. It's the way she watches me for a split second longer than she needs to. Like she's trying to commit me to memory in case I do anything stupid.

I wait a good forty minutes after the front door closes until I get out of bed. Quickly showering, I pull on a pair of black jeans and a matching jumper, throw my hair into a ponytail and make my way out of the house.

Seeing a baseball cap hanging on the wall I pick it up and slip it on as the door slams shut behind me. It's not like I'm planning on doing anything wrong today, but I didn't particularly want anyone to commit me to memory either.

The bus was ten minutes late and I find myself crushed between commuters as we follow the route towards Isabella's office. There's no worry of bumping into her, once she clocks in for the day she doesn't emerge until her working hours are complete.

In an effort to draw luck from the universe, I let several people disembark from the human constraints of the bus before I follow suit. What goes around comes around after all.

There are a couple of benches at the far end of the square outside her building and I choose the one that's partially obscured by a coffee truck.

I make sure to order a drink before sitting down, that way if anyone were to recognise me I'd just be a woman out for some fresh air and caffeine, waiting for her sister to take a rare lunch break. It was a feasible lie and one I could easily follow through with. I had only stayed home with a headache after all. Isabella would find it totally plausible that I'd hunt out her company once I felt better. She knows how much I love her.

But it's not Isabella I'm keeping my eyes peeled for this morning.

It's Andrew.

Sooner or later that snake will emerge from his basket and I'll follow him. If he believes he's operating without a witness he's more likely to give something away.

Look, it's not like I'm expecting him to lead me to his stash of murder weapons or anything but he's bound to do something suspicious I can use to get Isabella to see the truth. At the moment she just thinks I'm delusional, that paranoia has its grip on me once again. But I'm not and it doesn't. Andrew is a bad man and it's up to me to prove it.

I sit outside for an hour before he comes into sight. An hour of people-watching and daydreaming. In fact, I'm so busy eavesdropping on a couple's hushed argument that I nearly miss him. Thankfully for me though as they step to the side, out of my line of sight, that's when I catch his silhouette walking towards a side street.

Taking care to throw my cup away, I don't want to litter after all, I begin to follow him, remaining at a reasonable distance at all times. Once or twice he nearly catches sight of me as we weave across roads and pedestrian crossings but thankfully each time I've managed to make myself invisible.

I bent down to tie my shoe, turning my head backward as though someone had just called out to me and once I even joined in with a group of friends as they laughed at a joke. That moment in particular had been rather humiliating. They'd all stopped and stared at me, confused as to my presence. I'd walked away wordlessly because really, how could I possibly explain my actions?

It had all been worth it though. About five minutes ago Andrew had disappeared inside a block of flats.

A block of flats that I know for a fact is not his place of residence.

From the run-down state of the building's exterior, I'd hazard a guess that he wasn't visiting a lover. He struck me as a man who always punched above his weight, never below it.

Twenty minutes passed before he emerged from the doorway again, this time with a package in his hands. Drugs? Could Andrew be selling drugs on the side? Is that what he was doing in there, picking up supplies?

I don't know a lot about drug dealing, but twenty minutes feels about right to me for a transaction of that size. It was a large parcel, bound carefully in brown paper with string tying its edges. He was carrying it very carefully under his armpit with one hand upon it at all times. If I could just get it away from him then I could finally get Isabella to see the truth about him.

Oh God.

What if he'd been supplying drugs to Samantha?

Maybe that's why he had her medical records. So he could exploit her illness and provide her with her drugs of preference.

That made sense.

That's what it had to be.

Andrew was a drug dealer who had the sense to do his research before finding his clients.

Just as I've made up my mind that I'm going to barge into him and grab the parcel he sticks a hand out and hails a taxi.

No.

No.

No.

He can't disappear. Not when I'm so close to finding out the truth.

I'm about to hail a taxi of my own when a strong arm pulls my hand down. I turn round with a shock. "Where are you going?"

It's Inspector Coulson, standing behind me, his hand still on my arm as he holds it to my side. His hair is slick with rain and that's when I feel the dampness of my clothes. That's when I spot the sea of umbrellas around me. The rain is torrential, and I hadn't noticed. So caught up in my pursuit of Andrew.

Maybe Isabella's right to worry.

"Shall we get you inside?" he asks, now letting go of my arm as his eyebrows knit together in concern. I can see why Isabella is interested in this man. His face is lovely to look at, not perfect due to the bend in his nose, but still lovely.

I'm too embarrassed by my actions to speak so instead I just nod. He places my hand through the crook of his elbow and leads me into a nearby cafe. He leaves me sitting at a table, still mute, and I notice the way he keeps turning around to check I haven't wandered off somewhere whilst he queues up to get us a drink.

I'm leaving a small puddle on the floor around my feet as my shoes release some of the moisture they've been holding onto for the last forty or so minutes. How did I not notice the storm? How is that possible?

The thing is, I already know the answer, it's happened to me before. Back when my mental problems started to rear their head.

It was at our parent's funeral of all places. I was sitting next to Isabella, which was making my skin itch, and I couldn't stop obsessing over their accident. As the hymns swelled up around me, I was reliving every moment since they left for dinner that night.

The argument I'd overheard.

The arrival of their friends.

The detached look on Isabella's face when the door knocked and two police officers had to break the news of their deaths to us.

There'd been a display of candles instead of flowers around the top pews where we were sitting, and I watched the flames pulsate with the collective breaths of the congregation as they shared their sorrow over our loss. Sending their love up to the rafters of the church as though a few paltry lyrics could encompass all my parents meant to them. And who knows, maybe to them it could.

To them, my parents had been friends, colleagues, siblings, children. To me they were everything. They were the people who'd raised me. Who'd shaped me. Who'd held my hand as I took my first steps, who patiently sounded out each word alongside me as I learnt to read. They were my entire world and to lose both of them in one go, well, it was just too cruel to contemplate.

Isabella called out in shock and it briefly awoke me from the fuzz of grief that had descended upon me. I can remember turning to look at her, it was probably the first time I'd truly looked at her since the night we'd had the news - back then I'd preferred solitude to her company - and she looked so scared as she bent down and began hitting me on the leg with a bible.

Turns out I'd knocked a candle over and the leg of my trousers had caught fire. I hadn't noticed the burning sensation. It hadn't existed to me until Isabella pointed it out and now something similar had happened. I hadn't noticed the storm until it had been pointed out to me. This was a very bad sign indeed.

James places the coffee on our table, slipped off his jacket and placed it around my shoulders. He was kind as well as handsome, my sister really was in trouble if she thought she could resist her attraction to him.

"May,' he begins gently, as though dealing with a clinically insane inmate, "what were you doing out in that weather?"

I weigh up my options because I'm sure that whatever I tell him will end up back with my sister, and decide to just lay the truth out before him. After all, he is a police officer, surely he'll be able to appreciate my suspicions about Andrew.

So I tell him about the medical records I found. The file. Andrew's line about having a dossier on me. The flat he visited. The parcel he was so protective of. I even confess to the fact that I've spent my morning somewhat stalking the man.

And James listens.

He genuinely listens. Interjecting with small questions where appropriate and making all the correct noises and nods.

And it feels so good to talk to someone who's actually hearing me. Who cares about what I have to say.

My relationship with Isabella is more than a little one-sided, always has been, but it's only now that I feel like it's becoming clearer to me that it shouldn't be like that. I should matter to her as much as she matters to me.

Once I finally finish talking we sit in silence for a while. Both nursing our coffees, regarding the other. I'm waiting for him to shut down my suspicions the way my sister had. To give me a logical explanation for everything I don't quite understand.

He doesn't though.

Instead, he pulls out a notebook from his pocket.

"Do you think you can remember where the flat was?"

I groan at his question, I don't know the area in the slightest and given my lack of awareness for anything other than Andrew himself it's unlikely.

"That's okay. Maybe when the rain slows I can walk you back towards the offices and you can point it out if you remember." He sounds patient, I hope he is.

Looking out of the window I can see that the storm is finally passing, and it seems that at least for now Inspector Coulson is willing to look into Andrew.

"What will you do?" I ask.

"Once I have an address I can have a word with a few people, see if it's a place of interest at all and then we'll go from there."

"Will you tell Isabella?"

"No. Not for now. If we don't find anything out then we'll have worried her for nothing."

"Good. And, thank you."

"There's no need to thank me. Your sister asked me to keep an eye on you, to look out for you, and I'm happy to do it." He smiles at me and I return the favour. Perhaps one day we'll smile at each other across their wedding table. I'd like that. I feel like James would make a good brother-in-law.

"Well still, thank you."

He looks out of the window and then stands, offering me his arm once again. We walk out of the cafe together and the sun begins to peek around the clouds. Everything is going to be okay. I'm not alone in this anymore.

"Just promise me one thing May. Leave all of this with me now, all you need to worry about is spending time with your sister."

I nod my head, believing with my whole heart that this is a promise I will keep. Once Isabella is home tonight I'll suggest we put on a movie and chill out together. And then tomorrow or perhaps the next day I'll head home. I don't need to worry about Isabella, James is taking care of her now.

Then he says something that causes all of the contentment in my body to evaporate, and he stops walking to look at me directly as he speaks.

"At least those messages have stopped now though, eh?"

Chapter Fifteen - Isabella

I really shouldn't be in Andrew's office.

And I definitely shouldn't be snooping through his drawers. But it's his own fault really.

If he'd been here when I came down to talk to him, then curiosity would never have gotten ahold of me. I've tried calling him twice and both times I've been sent to voicemail. Andrew has never ignored my calls, not once in our working relationship. He's always there at the end of the line whenever I need him, it's been that way since the day we met. But not today.

Today he's out running a 'personal errand' according to our shared calendar. Why he chose today, of all days, to spend time tying up his loose ends I don't know. My campaign for party leadership is on the rocks and my campaign manager is off lollygagging God knows where. So yes, it's entirely his fault that my irritation has left me rifling through his paperwork.

I'm trying to find the files May is so paranoid about. To prove to myself that she's just blowing it out of proportion, but no matter where I look I can't find the paperwork she described. Perhaps Andrew has hidden the files more securely now. Or maybe he left them with her on purpose.

I wouldn't put it past him. He has a cruel streak and messing with May's stability seems like something he'd enjoy. The closer he pushes her to the edge, the less options I had left to help her. I'll need to speak to him about that afternoon again, to find out what really happened.

Pulling a notepad across the desk in frustration at my lack of success, I root around in his desk tidy for a pen and my fingers find a memory stick. Now why would Andrew hide a memory stick amongst his stationary?

Granted, I know not everybody is like me and has a time and a place for everything, but Andrew is not a great lover of chaos either. Why is this USB stick not in his top drawer with the others I see him using regularly? What makes this worth hiding? Without questioning my motives too deeply I push the stick into my pocket and leave Andrew a note.

It's the right call.

I write. Not wanting to embellish any further on what I mean, lest prying eyes stumble across the note.

Andrew would know exactly what decision I was referring to and by the end of the day the press would have the photographs of my competitor wrapped in the arms of his vastly younger mistress.

To be fair, I don't know why I've been so resistant to publishing them. I guess I wanted to win under my own merit rather than because of a man's failings, but needs must I guess.

I will do more good for our party than he would, and that's what politics is all about - doing good. Or at least that's what it should be about.

Too many of my colleagues are only interested in how their seats can serve them or, by proxy, their friends. Having contacts in hedge funds can be useful when your voting decisions can help tank the pound.

I've turned a blind eye to too many brown paper envelopes being passed between the back benches. When I'm in charge though all of that will stop. I will finally have the power to make it stop. Once, when I was newly in my role, I did try to bring it up to my senior colleagues. They all but patted me on the head and sent me on my way. It was nothing to worry about, they told me. They were wrong.

My constituents voted for me because they trust me, and it's because of that trust, I'm making the decision to blow apart a family with a series of candid photographs. It's all for the greater good.

Satisfied that Andrew will take care of business when he returns from his magical mystery tour, I make my way back towards my office. Being sure to greet everyone I pass with a smile and a nod, it's important that I'm well-received, that I'm liked, that I'm different from all of my peers.

That's what we've built my whole career around, that I'm a nice politician. You would think it wouldn't be that much of a driver for voters and yet it is. The general public prefers to vote for someone with charisma, someone who they can see themselves having a conversation with, someone who has their best interests at heart. And so that's who I've become, under Andrew's careful guidance.

I hold babies, I laugh at jokes and I make sure to shake every hand offered to me. It's no wonder I enjoy my solitude at the end of each day. The chance to be my true self. Constantly playing the part of the 'nice girl' is exhausting, but it will all be worth it when I'm Prime Minister, when I get invited to have an audience with the King at Buckingham Palace. When I get the final say on decisions that will shape the country.

I close my office door gently and lean against it, allowing my face to morph back into its neutral position. Sitting at my desk I plug Andrew's memory stick into my laptop and wait for it to load. Mindlessly I scroll through its contents, to find that it's photographs of James.

James ordering coffee.

James speaking to his colleagues.

James smiling at somebody's joke.

So, Andrew is building a dossier on Inspector Coulson. That's to be expected I suppose, he has always been a little protective of who I allow into my life.

I read through the notes he has jotted down, a full background check on my Inspector. The tale of a young boy, raised by two careless alcoholics who left home as soon as he was legally able. Thankfully his parents passed on liver failure shortly afterwards, his demons were laid to rest many years ago. There's nothing troubling in here though, something that probably irritated Andrew but brings great comfort to me.

James is actually one of the good guys.

If Andrew hasn't been able to dig up any dirt on him then that means his hands are clean. It means I'm free to indulge in this flirtation a little more. Andrew is more thorough than Scotland Yard, mostly due to his connections, so if his network came up blank then it means there's nothing to worry about.

I know Andrew won't approve, I know he'll tell me I'm risking a lot but I also know that he'll see my side of the argument. If things work out with James he will be the perfect partner for everything my future holds. The public will adore him. He's handsome, kind and charismatic, they won't be able to resist.

He'll bring in the blue-collar votes and we'll be the nation's sweethearts. It's such a shame that I have to paint such a picture in order for Andrew to trust my decision but the trust between the two of us is eroding slowly so I have no other choice.

I know that I can trust James. He's nothing like the men I've wasted my time on before. He is nothing like Marcus.

Then again, I suppose I thought I could trust Marcus when we first got together. If I'd known what he was really like I never would have let him into my life, let alone my bed.

It had all started with grand promises, as it always does, of meetings with his influential friends if I just agreed to go out for one drink with him.

That one drink led to dinner which led to the best sex of my life. And all of that led to a relationship that spanned two years and a lifetime's worth of broken promises.

The meetings that he'd first used to lure me into socialising with him did eventually transpire, but it turned out that his influential friends were more of the criminal variety than political.

Not that it wasn't interesting making their acquaintance, even criminals vote, but it wasn't as beneficial to my fledgling career as he'd let me believe. I should have known straight away that Marcus was the kind of person who promised good and delivered sub-par.

It was that way throughout our time together. Money lent was never returned, and promises of a big investment opportunity always round the corner.

Flirtatious glances were always innocent, he only had eyes for me. A request I made for help with campaigning was left unanswered - the list goes on and on. Honestly, looking back I'm surprised he was the one who left and that it wasn't the other way round. But I was blinded to his lies and his ego because I loved him. Warts and all. I justified, to myself, every time he let me down. He was a busy man, he was a charming one - nothing that annoyed me was his fault. Like many women before me, I let my life be ruled by a mediocre man.

I didn't come out of the relationship totally empty-handed though. Quite a few of our mutual acquaintances chose me over him, hitching their wagon to a more prominent horse. Not that I mind. The more people I have in my corner the better.

But now I have the chance to be with a real man, one I can trust with my heart. It's been so long since I felt ready to take that risk again but James will be worth it. I know he will. With this optimism in mind, I pick up my phone and type out a text to him:

Lunch tomorrow? X

As far as I'm concerned the mysterious penman has ended their campaign and we're now free to move our relationship away from the professional into the personal.

There's no longer a conflict of interest. I've no doubt that James' thorough investigation into the notes has frightened off whatever idiot was behind them.

It turns out, as it often does, that Andrew had made the right decision when he placed the call with the police about them. Because that decision had brought James into my life and I wasn't about to let an opportunity like him slip out of my hands.

I watch the screen as three dots appear and then disappear.

Appear.

Disappear.

What's taking him so long?

I know I should probably say no, but I'd love to.

I feel relieved that his delayed response has been down to his conscience rather than his disinterest in me.

Not tomorrow though. I need to come in and talk to you and I'd prefer to make our first date special. So how about dinner at the weekend?

Mild irritation bristles across my skin, I'd had my heart set on starting things with him tomorrow. Still, I should play it cool, I shouldn't let him know how much I wanted him.

Sounds good. I'll see you tomorrow.

I suppose all is not lost though. I'll be sure to make a real effort with my appearance tomorrow - whet his appetite for the weekend. I need to make sure he wants me as much as I want him.

That's the only way a relationship between the two of us will work. I'm a hard woman to love, I know that. If things get serious between the two of us eventually I'll have to let my mask slip and show him the real me. The quiet introverted me.

So my best chance of getting him to stick around after that revelation was to make sure he was as physically attracted to me as possible before I let him see the real me.

That way it would be harder for him to turn and leave when the truth comes out. Because the truth has a tendency to reveal itself eventually, that's something I'm beginning to learn.

I'm not intending to tell May about my date. She's too erratic at the moment. She'd probably try to talk me out of it. Paranoid that my heart will get broken again.

Ejecting the USB stick from my laptop I toss it into my bin. It seems there are a few more things I need to discuss with Andrew.

Whenever he decides to grace me with his presence.

As though summoned by my thoughts I hear a cough and turn to see him standing in the doorway.

"We need to talk," he says ominously.

"Yes. We do." I reply, gesturing at him to shut the door.

Now is the time to pick my words carefully, there are quite a few things I want to settle between the two of us and I need to make sure he understands every one of them.

Chapter Sixteen - May

James hasn't outed me yet.

In fact, I'm not even sure he knows I'm behind the messages. He didn't expand anymore on his line about them stopping and I didn't press him. Instead we walked together, back towards Isabella's office and I stayed silent, under the guise of concentrating on retracing my steps.

I did manage to remember the flat I'd seen Andrew disappear into though. I was quite proud of myself for that. So was James. He scribbled the address down but I haven't seen him since he put me back on the bus that morning, so I haven't been able to ask him if he's found anything out about Andrew yet. At least he's on James' radar though, at least I'm not alone in my suspicions anymore.

I nearly turned down Isabella's offer to come to the office with her today, but just as I was about to make an excuse she took a call that was clearly Inspector Coulson. I could tell from the way her voice dropped to a more sultry tone and her cheeks blushed.

Needless to say I couldn't turn down the opportunity to catch up with him so I hopped quite willingly into her waiting car and even joined in with the small talk between her and the driver. There's a sense of positivity that's beginning to wash over me. It's been that way since James listened to my fears about Andrew. I guess this is what happens when someone believes in you.

That was a couple of hours ago though, and I've been stuck in a different side office this time. It's just as bland as the one I spent my afternoon in filing last time. Left with a laptop and a list of names to transpose into a system. I've mostly spent my time completing quizzes on Buzzfeed though, it turns out I'm more of an Ariel than a Cinderella so at least it hasn't been a total waste of a morning.

From the office they've put me in today, I have no way of spotting if Inspector Coulson, James, has arrived. As far as I can tell this is the only room down the corridor that's occupied, I haven't heard the sounds of anyone else moving around. Andrew clearly believes in hiding problems far away from watching eyes.

So I keep finding reasons to pop across to Isabella's office. I can tell she's getting fed up with my mindless questions, but I can't stop. Short of stealing her phone to get hold of his number I have no other way of contacting him than bumping into him in her office. And if I asked for his number that would only look suspicious.

The last time I snuck across to her office I found her and Andrew in the middle of a hushed conversation at the farthest point of the room, door slightly ajar. I'd gently knocked and waited to be called in. Isabella actually looked relieved at my interruption - perhaps there is trouble in paradise. Andrew had all but barged past me as he stormed from the room. Good. The less time he spent with my sister the better.

That was nearly two hours ago though, and so far I've managed to resist the urge to go back to her office since then.

Instead I make my way down to reception, if anybody is going to know who Isabella has had visit so far today it will be the front desk. For all I know, James has already been and gone and I've missed my chance to connect with him.

The thought of that quickens my steps as I move towards the lift. I can't have missed him. That can't happen. I need to speak to him.

Have I become obsessed with James?

Perhaps.

Is it for the greater good?

Perhaps.

After the correct amount of small talk between me and the receptionist I inquired after Isabella's visitors. Knowing that because I'm her sister they'll give me this information, believing that she won't mind me knowing. And she won't. So long as I don't do anything daft with it.

I have to fight the urge to turn and sprint back upstairs when he lets me know that Inspector Coulson has just arrived.

We must have just missed each other, damn it.

It would have been a lot easier to pull him aside before he stepped into my sister's office.

I'll have to come up with an excuse she'll buy into if I want to steal five minutes of his time. Isabella has never been very good at sharing, especially not attention.

So I force myself to keep my pace steady and try not to tap my foot impatiently as I wait for the lift to return to the ground floor to collect me.

Would it be quicker to take the stairs?

Probably not with the health of my lungs, I'll end up collapsing in the stairwell on my way up to the tenth floor. No. I'll be patient. The lift will be here shortly.

As though summoned by my good behaviour the doors in front of me open with a ping and I bash the button for my sister's floor, praying that James isn't in the other lift on his way to the exit. That would be some delicious irony.

Is that irony? I don't know. Maybe.

Calm down, May. Calm down.

My thoughts are racing and my inner monologue is beginning to lose sense. This has happened before. This is how it all started before.

The lift doors open and I take a large step out into the corridor, gulping down a few deep lungfuls of air. I must calm down. I must regain control of my brain. Feeling more sane I walk towards Isabella's door. It's ajar again and I peek inside before making myself known.

Isabella is leaning against her desk, James has his eyes upon her and Andrew has his upon the Inspector. It's like a tableau of lust and jealousy.

How have I never noticed Andrew's feelings towards my sister before? It's so obvious now. I wonder if James has picked up on it? Is that why he was so willing to listen to my suspicions? Was jealousy clouding his judgement?

I knock on the door and then open it, without waiting for an invitation. They all stop talking at once. It's pretty obvious what they've been talking about.

Me.

James has the good grace to look guilty, as though I've caught him with his hands in the biscuit tin. Isabella has that false smile on her face that she uses if a constituent asks her an awkward question, and Andrew….. well, Andrew is grinning at me like the cat who got the cream. Andrew is practically glowing with joy. If you wanted to paint somebody looking victorious then Andrew's expression in this moment is the one you would use.

My nerves are on edge as I take another step into the office, wondering what they've been saying about me, waiting to see who will speak first.

"Hello, May," James says, greeting me with a soft tone that doesn't match the tension in his features. Has Isabella told him about my past? Is that why he's behaving as though I've lost the plot?

Have I lost the plot?

I don't think I have. Not really anyway. It's not as bad as last time. Or the time before. At least I'm not hallucinating yet.

"Hello, Inspector Coulson," I reply, stretching out a hand towards him to shake. After all, as far as anyone else in the room is concerned this is the second time I've met him.

"We were just talking about you," Isabella is the first to tell me the truth. Just as I knew she would be. My little sister has always had a rather abrupt personality. She sees no point in beating about the bush when she has a point to make. It's what makes her such a thrilling watch in the Commons.

She's there at nearly every meeting, something her constituents love her for. Sometimes though, I wonder if she spends more time showboating in Parliament than she does actually serving the people who voted for her.

Then I remind myself that I shouldn't think such unkind thoughts about the woman I'm so proud of.

"Oh really, anything interesting?" I ask with a smile, as though I couldn't possibly have a clue what she's talking about.

"Yes, James said he bumped into you the other day when it was raining-"

"You'll have to narrow it down," I interject with what I hope is a good-natured jibe about the weather in our country. She smiles tightly. Patronisingly.

"He said you were wandering around without a coat!" Her voice raises at the end of her sentence, as though she's asking a question.

She's not though. She's making a statement and delivering a reminder to me that I must behave better. I must be more sensible.

"I know, it was a rather stupid decision, but when I left to pop out I could have sworn I saw the sun peeking out from behind the clouds. I guess I was feeling optimistic." The lie trips easily off my tongue, and I can tell from the relieved sigh of air that emanates from my sister's nostrils that I've said the right thing.

She doesn't want James to know about her sister's troubles. She doesn't want anyone to know. I'm an embarrassment—a liability.

But the way Andrew is smirking at me tells me that he knows. He knows all about my breakdowns, numerous as they seem to be. He knows about Isabella institutionalising me when things got too difficult for her. He knows every dirty secret my sister has kept protected for me. And I don't know what he plans to do with that information but I can't imagine it will be kind.

"Anyway, sorry for interrupting but I thought I'd check to see if you needed a coffee before I went to the cart downstairs?" I lie again, playing the part of the dutiful, and more importantly, sane sister.

"No, I'm okay, thank you," she replies. We're being so polite to each other it's making me feel nauseous. I nod my head and turn to leave, letting out a gut-pulling sneeze as I do so.

"Oh you poor thing, it sounds like you're coming down with a cold." She's doing her best to sound maternal and I suppose on the surface it's working. James smiles at her thoughtful nature, but it freezes on his face unnaturally as she unhooks a scarf from it's hook on the wall and passes it to me. "Here, wear this, keep yourself wrapped up."

She holds the scarf out towards me and I reach for it, painfully aware of James' gaze on my skin as I do so. Great, now I'm going to look like even more of a nutcase wandering around the office in a knitted scarf that quite frankly has seen better days.

"I'll walk down with you, May," James offers and I can feel Isabella's shoulders tighten as he does so. She isn't ready for him to leave yet but how can I make him stay? Especially when this is exactly what I've waited all day for. "I was on my way out anyway."

He says goodbye to my sister and Andrew, and we walk in silence together towards the lift. I'm painfully aware that Isabella will be listening out to catch our voices in conversation, but I'm not sure why he's keeping his words locked away.

He gestures for me to step into the lift before him, I push the button for the ground floor and the doors close.

"I'm sorry about that. I didn't mean to tell her about the other day," he begins.

"Have you looked into Andrew?" I interrupt.

I'm not in the mood to play the forgiving woman right now. Our time together is limited and I need answers. Besides, it isn't a large betrayal in the scheme of things. The scarf is rubbing up against the skin on my neck, causing an itch and I remove it now I'm out of Isabella's eyeline. James watches me curiously as I do so.

Perhaps he's wondering why I even accepted the gesture if I had no intention of following through and wearing the damn thing. He has yet to realise that life is just easier if you agree with Isabella.

"The address of the flat is one a few of my colleagues have heard of before."

I knew it. I knew Andrew was up to no good.

"But I ran a full background check on him, he's as clean as a whistle May. I don't think he's done all the things you think he has."

It seems I don't have the ally in him I was relying on.

"I think you're underestimating him," I retort.

"I'm not. Believe me I'm not. I even tried to talk to Isabella about something just now before he interrupted. She didn't seem keen on my idea though."

"What idea?" I ask.

"I think he's behind the notes."

I nearly laugh. The one thing he thinks Andrew is guilty of is the one thing I know he couldn't possibly be.

"It would make sense, you know? It keeps him as an important figure in Isabella's life? Reminds her of how loyal he is, given the lengths he's gone to in order to uncover the culprit."

The lift dings open and I step out into the lobby, making sure to turn my path towards the coffee cart on the off chance Isabella is watching us on the cameras.

"There's no way Andrew is behind the notes," I reassure.

"I'm just saying it's not beyond the realms of possibility."

This time I can't hold back the snort of laughter bubbling up from inside of me.

This man knows nothing.

He can't help me protect my sister.

"What's so funny?" James looks annoyed now and I can't say I blame him. He's been nothing but kind to me.

I stop walking. There's only one way I'm going to get him to drop this train of thought and take my suspicions seriously. Only one thing that I can tell him that will force him to start digging around in Andrew's past to find the truth.

"I sent the notes James. It was me."

He doesn't give me time to explain.

His face falls and he looks at me in disgust. There are no probing questions from him, just disappointment. That's worse somehow.

Before I can reach out to him, to make him stay and listen to my explanation he has backed away from me.

With one last look in my direction he heads for the building's exit.

Why did I think my confession would win him over?

What kind of logic had I applied, in that exact moment, that made me believe there was any other outcome than the one I'd received?

Shit.

Chapter Seventeen - Isabella

May locked herself in her room last night under the guise of feeling under the weather. She didn't even come downstairs for dinner, which is most unlike her, as my sister never turns down the opportunity to spend time with me.

I know it's because she's avoiding having 'that' conversation with me.

The one where I confront her about her little walk in the downpour. I don't buy her excuse that she was being optimistic about the weather, nobody is optimistic about the weather in this country. It's as grey and gloomy here as it's ever been so any tale she tries to spin about believing otherwise will be a lie.

I can't believe she'd be so foolish - it's a clear sign that she's no longer thinking straight, that it's all getting too much for her.

The May I know is always sensible, always concerned with what others think about her. It's what makes her such a reliable person in my life. No matter what offers were thrown her way she never stepped out of line, always protecting me and my reputation. It's how I know Andrew's wrong when he says I can't trust her anymore, when he tries to get me to see that I'm running out of options.

Because there will always be options where May is concerned. I've brought her back from the brink before and I can do it again.

My phone beeps and I can see from the screen that it's a text from James. I don't open it immediately. I'm a little put out by the way he practically raced out of my office after May earlier. He's never seemed that desperate to talk to me.

It ignited a little bit of jealousy inside of me, I'm not ashamed to admit to that. But I know I have no real worries about the two of them. For a start, I am certain James is interested in me - why else would he want to take me out this weekend?

Plus I've seen the way his eyes linger on my legs whenever I cross them. Even if all that wasn't true, I know May. She would never engage with a man she knows I'm attracted to. That woman lives and dies by a moral code and I respect that.

So I decide to leave James on unread for the time being. A little waiting will do him good. It'll remind him where his interest should lie. Treat them mean and all that. Usually I wasn't interested in games, preferring to just lay my cards on the table with whomever took my fancy. Clandestine meetings hidden in hotel rooms that would quickly fizzle out were my usual MO, but James was different. He deserved my full repertoire.

"May?" I call out to her softly through the door, gently knocking.

I pause and wait for a response, or even a noise of life to escape from inside the room but there's nothing. Not even the rustle of a duvet as she turns in her bed. For all intents and purposes May doesn't exist right now, and I have to respect that.

If I push she might turn on me, might start blaming me for all manner of things and then the situation would spiral, and I might finally have to concede to Andrew that he's right about her. That she's too far gone this time for me to save her.

Walking back downstairs I settle on the sofa, television on low to give the sense that I'm watching something when in fact I'm a million miles away. I'm no longer in my living room. No longer worried about my sister and the danger she might present. I'm somewhere warm and calm and quiet. Somewhere I'm completely in control.

My hand reaches out for someone's arm, grasping it harder than I expected. A shiver of excitement runs through me as I look into their eyes. I'm done being side-lined. This is where I take charge.

I can feel the mindless smile take hold of my face as I drift away down memory lane but my thoughts are interrupted by a ringing. With a start I realise it's my phone, Andrew's name flashes up on my screen and I roll my eyes. I don't have the capacity to talk to him right now. I hit the divert button and send him to voicemail. If it's important he'll leave a message.

The phone rings again, and I answer it with a snap.

"What?" I bark down the line but barely let him answer my question.

"Andrew. You work for me, not the other way round." I hang up the phone and shove it under the sofas cushions where I no longer have to think about it. The man needs to stop being so incessant.

He may have been good to me all of the years we've worked together but that doesn't entitle him to my time whenever he pleases. Our relationship has become too unprofessional recently, blurring the lines of employer and employee and clearly he's taken my kindness for granted.

Tomorrow I'm going to revoke his access to my private calendar, the one where I keep my personal appointments. That should hopefully send a clear message that his extra interest in my life is no longer welcome.

A dark thought crosses my mind.

What if it's Andrew sending the anonymous messages? What if this is his way of making himself seem valuable to me?

It's not a completely outlandish idea.

He was the first person I contacted when I found that note in my office. The first person I knew I could rely on. If you add into that the message about May and his disdain for her, then it makes even more sense. He might have been hoping I'd send her away to keep her safe.

Yes.

There is a very real possibility that Andrew is behind the mysterious messages. And if that's the case, I have an even bigger problem on my hands than the breakdown of my older sister. Andrew is privy to too many of my secrets. If I don't play this right, then he could destroy me.

Digging through the pillows, just moments after my mini-tantrum, I retrieve my phone. There's two more missed calls from Andrew but no voicemail. The more I ignore him the quicker he'll get the message that I don't want to hear his petty theories about my sister and our lives. Instead I open the text James sent me earlier.

I'm not sure I can make it this weekend now. Can I let you know?

This doesn't make any sense. Last night he'd been insistent that he take me out on a real date, that he wanted to make it special, and now he wanted to take a rain check? What could possibly have happened in the last twenty-four hours that has caused him to backtrack on our plans?

May.

Everything was fine until he came to speak to me about May. To tell me about her little walk in the rain.

To confide in me his concerns about her mental state.

Could it be that James doesn't want to get involved with me because of the baggage May brings with her? Because he doesn't want to date a woman with a 'crazy' sister?

I thought better of him, thought he was different to Marcus, but perhaps all men are a let-down.

I wouldn't stand for it though. Nobody disrespects my sister. Not Andrew and certainly not a man I've only recently met. If he thinks May is too much for him, then he's not enough for me. I love my sister and I will stand by her until the bitter end.

Why?

I reply. Wanting to see if he has enough of a backbone to be honest with me, and if he does, then I'll be able to engage in an argument. I have one itching to go right beneath my skin and it would be a relief to let it loose on someone.

The world irritates me so much. There are so many wrongs out there and the way people treat each other is one of the main ones. I thought James was a compassionate individual. He'd come across that way whilst dealing with my case. But maybe he's only compassionate when it suits him, like so many other people.

May's problems are just a temporary blip. Nothing serious is going to come of them, and if she stumbles too close to breaking, then I'll have to arrange another stay for her in the Sanctuary. It worked last time and it will work again. I'll even pay extra to ensure she has the same care team for her particular needs.

Something has come up about your case. I can't tell you about it yet, but I will soon. And then we can go out for dinner.

It seems like a fairly honest response and I toy with the idea of placing my faith in his words. There might be things going on behind the scenes that I'm not privy to. Somebody may have given him a tip off about the messages and he's putting my safety above his want to be together. But would that be naive of me? To trust him when he says that's all that's going on.

I know my life is a lot to handle. Even when May is safely sequestered away in her own home, it is a lot. There are never ending social functions, you can never truly speak your mind outside of your own home and you have to mistrust every acquaintance.

Maybe it isn't May and her mental state that's causing him to withdraw, maybe it's just me and the circus I reside in. If that's the case then I can't be mad at him, I'd understand his reluctance to become a part of the 'Isabella show.' Sometimes I'd love to jump off the hamster wheel myself, even if just for one afternoon.

But this is the path I've chosen for myself and I will follow it through to the end, otherwise everything has been for nothing.

Sounds good to me.

I keep my text casual, not wanting him to know that I'm second guessing every character of his messages. I'm letting myself spiral. I should just take him at his word. He isn't judging me or May. He's just doing his job.

I had a thought tonight.

Am I really going to confide in him about my worries about Andrew? That would be a betrayal to the working relationship we've built up over the years. Not to mention if he ever found out it would result in a situation I'd rather avoid, a situation that wouldn't end well for either of us. That's the problem with working with someone for so many years, you both get tied up in each other's secrets.

?

He replies. No words, just punctuation. Others may be offended by this but I find it rather charming. I've always appreciated a forthright person. I pause, my fingers hesitating over the keyboard. This is the moment I decide whether I can trust him or not, whether I trust Andrew or not.

I'm really looking forward to our date.

I chicken out. There would be too much to lose should Andrew learn of my suspicions that he's behind the notes. I can't risk word getting to him. I don't honestly know how he'd react.

A few weeks ago I could have just confronted him but recently he's changed. Or I have. I'm not sure. I just know that May's visit and subsequent paranoid behaviour has altered the relationship between myself and my trusted campaign manager. Something in the air has shifted between us and I worry about what that might mean for our future.

Trudging up the stairs towards my bedroom I give one final knock on May's door.

"You're coming to the office with me tomorrow, May. I thought we could take a long lunch break together."

Usually the offer of some one-on-one time is enough to pull her out of any funk but the only thing that responds to me is silence. Deathly silence. I wish

I'd removed the locks on the doors when I'd bought the place, but they were an old-fashioned reminder of the life this house had before me. They added character to the place. Now I wish I'd ripped the doors from their hinges and replaced them with something generic the day I moved in. At least that way

I'd be able to walk into her room and physically see that she was alright. For all I know…

No.

No. She's never done anything like that before.

She wouldn't do that to me.

"May?" I knock harder this time, my knuckles sting with the force but panic has grabbed hold of me.

"May!" I repeat, this time raising my voice, hoping the panic within it will reach out to the part of her that's still sane. That still cares about me.

"Fine. I'll come with you tomorrow," she shouts back at me in response and a sob chokes in my throat. For a second there I thought I'd lost her. I thought she'd taken herself away from me forever. I'm so relieved to hear her voice that I could laugh.

"Goodnight, May," I call through the door and I'm not surprised that she doesn't reply. She wants to be alone to rest, and maybe some solitude will help bring her back to the sister I need her to be.

Chapter Eighteen - May

Don't trust Andrew.

My hands are shaking as I press send on my latest burner phone. I know I don't have much time before James comes clean to Isabella about my secret. So I have to use what time I have left to embed the seed of doubt about her assistant so deep into her brain that it might cause an aneurysm.

If she won't listen to me or James directly then maybe she'll take the word of a stranger above ours. I drop the phone into the clean toilet bowl, wait a few minutes then pull it out and hide it in the sanitary bin that's in the cubicle with me.

It was risky to send the message from within Isabella's office but I didn't have a choice. She's been following me around like a shadow since James told her about my little walk in the rain and it would look even more obvious if I sent it from the bedroom of her house. The only times I've been alone in the last twenty-four hours have been when I'm peeing or sleeping - it reminds me of my stints in the sanctuary.

Although at least there you were granted a bit of privacy after the medications round had been completed. They'd guide us all back into our private rooms, lock the door, and leave us unattended for a few hours whilst the effects kicked in. What I wouldn't do for a bit of forced solitude right now.

Lo and behold, as I exit the public bathroom, I find Andrew leaning against the wall waiting for me. I guess Isabella has a call and can't partake in guard duty herself.

He looks about as thrilled at the situation as I am and briefly, I consider telling him that he can leave. That I am not a danger to myself. But the man would never disobey a direct order from my sister; he loves her too much to do that.

"Come along then," he says to me, marching ahead. With a barely concealed sigh, I do as bidden. There's no point in trying to rebel right now as Isabella reminded me on the drive over she's just doing all of this for my safety. To prevent me from being committed again. To save me from myself.

To my paranoid ears, it sounded like more of a threat than a concern, but I let sleeping dogs lie. I've spent years of my life being told I can't trust my own mind and I'm in no position to start questioning that now. My sister just wants to protect me. That's all she's ever wanted.

Andrew walks me silently into a large office. There are awards hung on the wall, pictures of him shaking various politicians' hands and finally an oil painting of what I assume is his family home.

His office is a stark contrast to the neutral colour palette of my sister's. The desk, which of course is located bang in the centre of the room, is large and ostentatious. I think it might be walnut, but I've never concerned myself too much with the visual recognition of wood so I can't be sure. There's a large jet black monitor in the middle of the desk, accessorised with a pile of files and paperwork all properly placed on top of an intray.

Sometimes I wonder exactly how much work there is for Andrew to undertake. Surely he's just a glorified personal assistant? This office is set up to let me and anyone else who is allowed to enter know otherwise. Andrew is a powerful man. A busy one. One not to be crossed.

He gestures towards a small pop-up desk that's been placed haphazardly near the door, a fair stretch from the windows I assume my sister worries I'll throw myself from.

"More data entry. Just be quiet, that's all I ask." There is a part of me that respects Andrew for his honesty right now. He's not trying to pretend that babysitting a grown woman is a task he's grateful for. He doesn't appreciate my presence in his office. But I do.

As far as I'm concerned, I'm now sitting in the viper's nest, and if I'm going to prove to my sister that he isn't to be trusted before James blows my cover, then the answers I'm looking for are bound to be squirrelled away in here. I just need to wait for him to get a call, or take a bathroom break, and I'll be free to snoop to my heart's content.

Unfortunately for me, the man has a steel bladder. It's two hours later when he finally stands from his desk and excuses himself. There's a moment where I see him consider asking me to follow him. After all, he isn't supposed to take his eyes off me.

He thinks better of it though. I've felt his irritation at my presence grow with every minute I've spent in my corner typing as quietly as possible. I haven't wanted to give him any reason to palm my care off to somebody else. I'm also banking on the fact that he'll be fighting that urge as well due to his desperate need to consistently prove his value to my sister.

I wait until I can no longer hear his footsteps and leap from my chair. Hopefully, somebody along his journey will stop him and cause a delay but I have to work quickly. Luck isn't always on my side.
Standing in front of his desk I'm not quite sure what I'm looking for. A selfie of him over Samatha's dead body? I mean sure that would be the perfect evidence

but I'm quite sure the man isn't daft enough to do that. Trying each of the desk drawers first I find them all disappointingly unlocked, their contents containing nothing of note.

Next, I flick through the paperwork on his desk, again dull as dishwater. Before I can try to gain access to his computer I hear his voice approaching as he speaks to one of his colleagues.

As quietly as I'm able I make my way back towards my corner, sit down and continue typing. When he re-enters the office I notice him taking a quick scan of the surroundings. As though he knew I'd have been snooping. When a look of relief washes over his features I curse myself, there is something in this room he doesn't want me to find. I just haven't found it yet.

Still, there's half a day left here. Eventually, he'll have to leave me alone again. And when he does, I'll be sure to go through this room with a fine toothed comb. I remind myself to be careful though. I'm letting my suspicions about him, and my desperate need to prove my point to my sister, override a very simple fact. If Andrew truly is a murderer, then I need to make sure I keep myself out of his crosshairs.

I keep myself busy with my workload and make sure to only speak when spoken to. Which isn't very often at all. Mostly Andrew just wants somebody to nod along as he thinks out loud, and I'm in no position to stir the pot. If he was as mad as I believe him to be, then now would be the perfect opportunity for him to 'deal with me.' After all, with the way my sister is behaving it wouldn't be a complete surprise to hear I've thrown myself from a window or taken a letter opener to my arteries. My hand automatically rubs my throat at the thought.

She would believe it. I know she would. However, never in the history of my mental health, have I ever tried to or even expressed a desire to hurt myself. But people who don't suffer from mental health problems tend to tarnish us all with the same brush: crazy is as crazy does, after all.

And what about the Inspector? Would James believe I've thrown myself from the building knowing that I'm the one behind the notes?

Maybe he'd think it was guilt rather than depression that had forced me over the ledge. I was wrong to trust that man. I should have listened to the voice inside my gut, the one who told me he was a little too keen to take on my sister's case. The one who was wary of the interest he showed in her. He is not to be trusted and I'd made a terrible mistake in going against my instincts.

Andrew's scoff of derision pulls my attention. He's reading something on his computer and he finds the content of the document unbelievable. Maybe I should pry, just a little. If he's emotional, he might be vulnerable, and more likely to make a mistake I can exploit.

"What's wrong?" I ask, and for a moment he looks through me. I expect him to carry on with his task and act as though I've never spoken. He doesn't though. Instead, he folds his hands on top of each other and turns his body towards me. He's willing to converse.

"Samantha was writing a book about your sister, did you know?"

I respond by shaking my head. I've learnt enough about Andrew today to know he prefers a captive audience to an engaged one.

"Yet another snake was coming out of the woodwork to try and sabotage your sister's career and all the good work she's done. It's almost a pity the woman died. I'd have liked a day in court with her. So much slander in so few pages."

"It can't be that bad surely? They were only friends for a year."

Andrew laughs at my comment, then stares at me with something close to pity in his features.

"I always forget that you, well, that you forget."

"What do you mean?" I ask.

"Never mind. It doesn't matter. At least the book will never see the light of day now." He dismisses my question, and although I want to press him further I have to keep reminding myself of the precarious position I'm currently in. One quick shove through the window and he could kill me off without too many questions.

"Well, that's something, I suppose," I add, knowing that our brief conversation has come to its natural end. He's still staring at me though, and I'm uncomfortable with his attention.

"May, I know our relationship has been difficult so far. I just want you to know that everything I do is for your sister. I only have her best interests at heart." This is awkward. Is this his attempt at trying to connect with me? Or is he subtly letting me know how far he's willing to go to keep his word? I'm so conflicted that I can't find the right words to respond.

Then, the reason for his sudden heart-to-heart comes walking into the room. Isabella. Of course, that's why he spoke those words. This way he's won favour with her, and he now has weight to dismiss any of my concerns if I were to bring them to her attention. He'd tried to make amends with me, she'd heard him, and I'd left his kindness hanging in the air.

Bastard. Always one step ahead of me.

"I thought we could travel home together if you like?" she asks, behaving as though she hasn't heard Andrew's little speech. She has though, I can tell from the way she's looking at him.

"Sure," I reply, knowing I have very little choice in the matter.

"Isabella, could I have a word?" Andrew asks, then shoots a pointed look in my direction. "Alone."

"Can't it wait?" she asks, clearly wary of letting me out of her sight. He shakes his head and she sighs. "Okay, fine. May, can you wait for me outside?"

I do as I'm asked and pull the door to a close behind me. Part of me wants to press my ear up against its wooden frame, to steal the words from them they're so desperate to hide from me.

I fight the urge though, being caught eavesdropping on the two of them will only make my sister worry about my sanity further, and let Andrew know that I'm suspicious about him. Neither of which I can risk.

It's a good ten minutes before Isabella emerges, looking far angrier than she had when I left the room. Had the golden boy stepped out of line and upset her? I hope so. Then I can exploit her irritation for my own gains. Maybe if she's realising that Andrew isn't infallible she'll be more open to hearing my theories about him, and Samantha's death.

Managing to hold my tongue in the car was more difficult than I'd anticipated. Isabella kept trying to draw me into meaningless chit-chat when all I wanted to do was grab her by the shoulders and shake her until she listened to me. Is that a normal reaction? I don't know. I don't know anything anymore.

I do know that Andrew is trouble and I need to rescue my sister.

As soon as we step through the front door all of my words spill out into the space between us. She stands there patiently as I explain about Andrew's feelings for her and what they've driven him to. I tell her about Samantha and how he was the one supplying drugs to her. I tell her about the flat he disappeared into.

All the while, as I bare my soul before her she stands still. Barely breathing as her skin takes a paler shade. My words have shocked her. I don't blame her. I'd be taken aback to learn that somebody I trusted so much was a killer too.

"Have you been taking your medication?" is the first thing she asks me and that's when it hits me. She doesn't believe a word I've said. She hasn't listened to a single fact I've laid out before her and I have nothing more to convince her with. I've given her all I have and it's not enough. Maybe it will never be enough. She won't believe Andrew is guilty until she finds him with literal blood on his hands.

I allow her to guide me up to my room as sobs wrack my body. Nobody believes me. Nobody will listen to me. I'm completely helpless in this situation and there is no good way for it to end. Andrew will get away with everything and I will be left with nothing. My sister thinks I'm crazy. She's drawing away from me every day. I can feel it. There will be nobody left in this world who loves me.

I don't know what's going on anymore.

I don't know who I am anymore. I am taking my medication still, I really am, but it's clearly not enough anymore to keep my chemical imbalance in check.

Which is why I don't argue as Isabella sits on the side of my bed whispering soothing words to me. Perhaps she's right. Maybe I do need a break from reality again. Another stay in the Sanctuary could be the thing to save me from myself.

Chapter Nineteen - Isabelle

I'm starting to think that perhaps Andrew has been right about May all along. She's a danger to herself, and most likely to me at this point, and I should probably take action.

But she's my sister. I don't want to have to make that decision.

When he pulled me aside earlier as I was about to leave with May, he made sure to speak bluntly. Explaining to me that the situation had escalated too far out of control. To tell me that either I made the call or he did, but either way the call was going to be made.

I'd been mad when he said that. Incandescent with rage actually. Who did this man think he was to give me an ultimatum? I told him as much once he finished making his point. I may have even thrown a few items from my desk to ensure he felt the full force of my anger. I've been right all along. My relationship with Andrew has changed recently. It's been damaged by my sister's presence, and all that brings with it.

I wish things could have just stayed as they were: a weekly lunch date between the two of us, where nothing of interest was discussed and a daily telephone call whilst we cooked our evening meal. Why couldn't everything have just stayed as it was? Why do things have to change?

Whenever we spent too much time together it never seemed to end well.

Why did May have to come here and insert herself in my life?

What could possibly have driven her to turn up unannounced at my office that day?

May wasn't a spontaneous person. She always planned any travel weeks in advance. It's so out of character for her to have simply hopped on a train to come and surprise me.

Unless.

No. That's not possible.

In order to stop the thought that was trying to take up residence in my mind I stand from my seat at the kitchen counter and move towards May's handbag. My sister, as an accountant, is a meticulous receipt hoarder.

If there was anything untoward to find out about her time in my hometown it would be within her purse.

Even though I know I've tucked her safely up in her bed, I still glance around myself before I pull the zip open because this is a gross invasion of her privacy. And I'll soon find that it's a needless one. I'm certain May has nothing to hide from me.

And yet I pull out her purse and tip the contents onto the counter nonetheless.

A hotel receipt. Dated four days before her arrival at my office.

An open return train ticket dated and stamped for the same day.

A business card for a hot desk company near my office.

A telephone number, drawn in childish scribble on the back of a ripped piece of cardboard.

My sister has been lying to me.

Her visit was not spontaneous. She was staying here for at least four days before her arrival at my office.

She'd lied every one of those nights we'd shared our 'end of the day' call. There had been every opportunity for her to tell me the truth and she never had. She'd concealed her arrival here from me, but what I couldn't figure out was why.

May loves me. I know that. And she loves spending time with me. So why would she rob herself of that time by remaining hidden when she could have turned up at my door that first day? What could she possibly have been up to over those four days that required such deceit?

A shiver runs down my spine as I wonder if she'd sat at one of the desks across from my building and watched my comings and goings. Whether she booked that building specifically to keep an eye on me.

But why would she do that?

May is my sister, not my stalker. None of this makes any sense.

I pick up my phone and dial the number from the cardboard, a young male voice answers abruptly.

"Make and model?" He asks.

"Excuse me?" I stutter out in reply, which causes him to sigh loudly. I can hear the sounds of loud voices in the background behind him, wherever he is it sounds a lot more fun than where I am.

"What phone do you want?" He asks and I drop mine in shock. I listen as he calls out a few times before swearing to himself and hanging up.

Make and model. He thought I was calling up to order a phone. A burner phone.

I know what you did.

Those five words are a punch in the gut now. Now that I know my sister is the one behind them.

It's entirely possible, given her state of mind, that she doesn't remember exactly what it is she was referring to. But I know. I remember.

Turning to march up the stairs and confront her I pause to take a deep breath.

May is unwell. She's not herself. She probably doesn't even remember sending the notes or messages. It's entirely possible that she's almost suffering from split personalities. I don't need to panic just yet. I just need to get her well before it's too late. Before Andrew is proven right.

This has happened before. Back when our parents died. There was the incident at the funeral, where she burnt herself on the candles and hadn't even noticed. If I hadn't put her trouser leg out then her injuries would have been far more severe. She could barely even remember the incident the next day. Instead, she turned her attention to me.

I shudder at the memory. I hadn't been afraid many times in my life, but that day after the funeral I had been truly afraid of my sister and the things she was saying. There really had been no other option than to send her away to the Sanctuary at that time. I may have only been fifteen, but thanks to a few well-worded emails and our inheritance money, I was able to ensure May got the help she needed.

She emerged almost like the girl I'd known, just a little quieter, a bit more unsure of herself. But I guess that's to be expected when you've been told that your brain is lying to you. There wasn't another single whisper of an accusation from her lips or a statement of paranoia so I guess they did their jobs.
The second time I sent her there was after Chris.

Again, I'd really had no other choice. She'd turned up on my doorstep distraught. Sobbing about how she couldn't go on, she couldn't live with herself. She lashed out at me, striking me several times around the head before I had a chance to react. But once again the Sanctuary did its job and removed all the angry memories from her addled brain.

I didn't want to send her there again. I'm not sure how much more she can take. But the alternative doesn't bear thinking about.

With a sigh I turn from the hallway and walk back to the kitchen. I can't act rashly here, I have to weigh everything up and see if there's a more palatable solution to this problem.

Thankfully there's a bottle of wine in the fridge and I pull a glass from the cupboard and fill it to the brim. I give thought to putting the bottle away but decide not to fool myself into thinking I'm just going to have this one. Tonight is not a night to stay sober. There's too much to decide, and the edges of those decisions are rough and spiky. They're going to hurt. And I need to numb the pain.

May is convinced that Andrew has feelings for me. And that those feelings have made him a dangerous man capable of bloodthirsty deeds. She's partially right.

Andrew would do anything for me, has done anything for me, but it's not out of lust or love. It's because he's hitched his coattails to mine. My success is his success and we both know that when I'm holding the highest seat in politics that a world of opportunities will open to us.

Because of his loyalty I know I'll forgive him for becoming a mild irritation in my life. We've been through too much together for me to let him go anytime soon.

The wine warms my throat and I finish the glass in a succession of quick gulps, not hesitating before I pour another.

In the morning I'll gently confront May. I'll ask her about the messages and the hotel receipts and hopefully she'll have no memory of them. Because if she does remember doing all of that, then that means there's some malice simmering inside my sister that's aimed in my direction, and I can't have that. We've been through too much together for it to come to that.

I know what you did.

She'd written, she'd warned - but that was impossible. She couldn't remember. If she had remembered then we'd be in a lot worse state than we are now.

There really are very few options left available to me, and with Andrew's ultimatum hanging over my head, they were getting slimmer and slimmer by the minute. I'd love to live the next few weeks of my life fuelled by hope. Hope that she'll pull herself together and stop swimming in dangerous waters, but now I know she's lied to me, that she's the one behind the messages. That seems unlikely. She might be too far gone to rely on hope.

I could call her doctor and ask him to put her on a higher dose of medication. But if she's fracturing, then she's fracturing. Upping the dosage of her pills will only put a plaster over the problem. It's not a permanent solution and what do I do the next time her mind takes her to places she should avoid? I can only ask him to give her so much medicine. He does still have an oath to live by after all.

May thinks she's the one who always looked out for me, but if she knew I was in regular contact with her doctor, that I hand-picked her therapist and even put her forward for promotions at work, then she'd realise that I work just as hard as her when it comes to our sisterly bond. I have a finger on every one of May's pulses and she's never noticed. Not once has she realised just how hard I've had to work to keep her safe. How much money and time it has cost me.

That can't all be for nothing.

The Sanctuary is my second to last resort. But I don't feel good about it. The team they have there now aren't as malleable as the ones I've dealt with prior, and I won't have her receiving anything but the top care. Having finished the best part of the bottle I make my way quietly up the stairs. Despite how annoyed I am by her recent actions I can't deny that my sister is unwell, and therefore, I should let her rest as much as I can.

Especially considering all the decisions tomorrow must bring.

I shrug off my clothes, for once leaving them in a pile on the floor rather than folding them into the wash basket, and pull on a large t-shirt. It used to be Marcus', I only ever kept it out of spite as it used to be his favourite when we dated. I can't deny it's still comfortable though, even after this many years of general wear and tear.

Pulling the duvet up to my chin I snuggle down into its embrace, my head spinning a little from the alcohol consumed quickly. Yes, for now I'll let May rest and recuperate. Hopefully I'll be able to get some sleep too, and somehow in the morning the solution will have presented itself.

Hope.

Stupid hope.

Whether the answer comes to me in a dream or not, one thing is clear as I close my eyes.

Tomorrow will be a day of big decisions. I just hope I get to make them before Andrew steps in.

Chapter Twenty - May

When I wake up it's dark.

Isabella must have drawn the curtains after I fell asleep. Hoping some rest would help straighten my mind. And it has in a way. My thoughts are less emotional now. My tears have finally dried. Something isn't right. I've never felt this disconnected from the world, not even before my diagnosis.

Quietly I make my way from my bedroom towards the bathroom I share with my sister. I listen out for any sign that she's conscious but even from here in the hallway I can make out her not-so-gentle snoring. I am alone. For the first time in hours, I am alone. I relish the peace and quiet, the lack of eyes upon me and turn on the tap in the sink. Splashing cold water on my face I try to centre my thoughts.

What could possibly be happening to me right now?

Yes, I am suspicious of Andrew. Yes, I believe he's hurt, maybe killed somebody. But that doesn't explain the clawing paranoia at the base of my skull, the thud of my heartbeat as I worry, even now that something bad is coming for me. I've never been short of logic but I've been making rash decisions recently, worse and worse ones as the weeks have rolled by. So what could be causing it all?

In frustration at myself I throw my hand out, across the basins side and knock my prescription bottle to the floor. Freezing in position I wait to see if my sister wakes. The last thing I need is for her to find me upset with a bottle of pills. I won't be able to explain before she's on the phone to the crisis team. Although I imagine their company will be coming to see me in the morning anyway. There's no way Isabella hasn't called somebody. She worries too much to let me fall too far.

I pop a squat and pick up the bottle, regarding the pills inside. These tiny little things are supposed to help keep the monsters in my mind at bay, but they've stopped working. Clearly, they've stopped working. There's no other explanation for my mental state. I push down on the lid and twist, a motion so ingrained in my routine that I barely recognise I'm doing it. Shaking out a few pills into my hand I bring them up to my eye and really gaze at them.

They're different.

I don't know how to explain it but they are different. These are not the pills I have taken every morning of my adult life. They're slightly larger and they feel tacky to my fingertips. My usual medication is powdery, I know that because as I think of them my tongue feels dry. No. These are not my pills.

How did I not notice?

Because it's such an ingrained part of my routine I pay them no thought. Not usually.

But who would want to switch my pills?

Somebody who wanted me off the scene.

Andrew.

Of course, it was Andrew. He was the only other person with keys to Isabella's house.

I take a step towards her bedroom door, pills in hand, ready to confront her with cold hard evidence. And then I stop myself. This won't be enough. Somehow this won't be enough to convince her. I need more. I need to find more.

The flat.

If I can find these same pills inside that flat then I'll be able to prove the connection to Andrew. He won't be able to talk himself out of it. I'm pretty certain I can remember where it is, and it's only 10 p.m. so the night bus is still running into the centre. If I'm quick I can head over there, take some photos and be back here before Isabella wakes up in the morning. Hopefully, I'll have a chance to talk to her before the men in white coats cart me away again.

Making my way down the stairs I avoid the one that squeaks. It's not that I think my sister is a light sleeper, it's more I'm enjoying the silence around me. It's helping to keep my mind sharp and focused. The bus stop isn't a long walk from her house and I don't intend to stay too long at Andrew's flat.

How am I going to get in the flat?

Never mind, I'll work that out when I get there. I open the closet to the side of the front door, pulling out a pair of Isabella's trainers I slip them on, as grateful now for sharing a shoe size as I was when we were teenagers and I wanted to go clubbing. I'm about to leave when I remember being caught in the rain by James, and so I pull out the first coat I can lay my hands on.

It's a beautiful royal red, the coat she wore on her first day in Parliament. Briefly, I feel guilty as I slip my arms into it, then I reason to myself that so long as I was quick she'd never know I'd borrowed it.

How had James stumbled across me that day anyway?

It's highly unlikely that he'd been out for a daily walk in that weather. Even more unlikely in a city as big as this one that we'd be in the same place at the same time. I'd never questioned his presence that day but now, in the grips of clarity at what's been done to me, I'm starting to wonder about his entrance to our lives. Why was he so keen to investigate the messages Isabella had been receiving? I'd seen with my own eyes the very quick pace at which he'd walked to her office building, seen him sauntered away with a smile on his face after their first meeting. Had he engineered his place in her life just to sleep with her? It seemed a distinct possibility right now.

So now I had something else I needed to speak to Isabella about. But if I don't find the proof about Andrew then she certainly won't listen to my concerns about James. First things first, I have to find the source of these pills.

Thankfully she hadn't changed me into my pyjamas when she put me to bed, so I'm still wearing the clothes I'd worn to the office. That would save me a few strange looks from passers-by as I made my way through the city.

The bus takes a good ten minutes to arrive but thankfully there is a shelter for me to hunker down in. I also have the company of a few well-meaning bystanders, who'd had a few drinks, and their laughter keeps the chill from crawling into my veins.
We all board together and I sit towards the back, away from their little group, and stare out of the window as the world moves past me.

This is the right decision. It is the sensible one. Probably the first sensible one I've made in a while. It's been wrong of me to be angry at Isabella, and James, for not believing in my suspicions outright.

Would I instantly believe them if they came to me with something like this? No. Probably not. Because humans like the two of them crave logic. They need solid explanations. By the morning I will have that for them.

I press the button as I see Isabella's office in the distance, this is the easy part. Now I just have to trust in my memory and my feet to take me where I need to be. Thankfully, when James found me in the rain, he'd walked back with me so I'd seen the flat twice which should make it easier to remember.

Giving myself over to my instincts I begin to walk down roads, pausing when I'm not certain if I'm on the right track or not, letting my gut guide me in those moments until eventually, there it is in front of me. The flat.

Just as I'm about to take a step towards the entryway and try to blag my way inside there's movement behind the glass door. I freeze, staying within the shadows around me.

It's Andrew.

He looks both ways as he exits the entry, scanning the area for any witnesses. Satisfied he's alone he pulls the parcel in his arms closer to his chest and begins to walk away. It's the same package I saw him with the other day. I have to know what's inside.

All thoughts of getting into that building to prove that he's been messing with my medication evaporate. Whatever he's hiding is important to him, and I intend to get my hands on it as soon as possible.

Once again I find myself following Andrew down unfamiliar streets and paths, until eventually we come across a building site. I watch as he gently pushes against a few of the wooden panels surrounding it until one creaks and he slips through. He's been here before.

I count to twenty before following suit, taking care to move the panel softly to avoid a squeak. The air around us is silent and the noise would travel to his ears faster than I could run. I should call the police, that's what I need to do. That's the sensible decision here.

Putting my hands into the coats pockets I swear under my breath, I'm borrowing Isabella's coat. Of course my phone isn't there. How could I be so stupid? Because you aren't thinking clearly, May.

Because this man has been messing with your head, your medication, your sister.

Anger flashes through me at the unfairness of it all.

What have I ever done to Andrew to make him feel he has to break me? To break my relationship with my sister? Because it is broken, I can accept that now.

There is very little chance that Isabella and I will make it through this unscathed.

I have done nothing to him, other than show fits of jealousy towards him. Maybe that's all it takes to get on his wrong side.

He's a dangerous man. I shouldn't be here alone.

That voice in my head, the one that's born from self-preservation isn't as loud as the destructive one that's pushing me to step foot onto the building site though.

If I turn around and go home now, then all of this, the damage it's caused to my health and my relationship with my sister, will be for nothing. She will send me away again and he will get away with everything. I can't have that.

I'll stay hidden, just watch what he's up to, and then find someone with a phone. There's bound to be someone about who will let me use their phone to call the police. I just can't let Andrew out of my sight. Not yet.

Hiding behind a semi-demolished wall I watch as he crouches on the ground, the parcel out of view. I can't see what he's doing. Not from here.

Just as I'm about to be impulsive and move positions he stands. He wipes his hands on his trousers and begins to walk towards my hiding spot. Where's the package? What has he done with it?

I cower down, pressing my back as firmly against the wall as I'm able to as he passes by me. I'm so certain he can hear the beat of my heart that I expect him to stop in his tracks and turn towards me. He doesn't though. He makes his way back towards the fence panel and disappears back into the world.

Once again I count to ten, just to be sure he's really finished here, and then I emerge from my hiding spot, and take a step towards the ground he'd been kneeling in front of.

There's a freshly dug mound, but it's not very deep. Is this where he leaves the drugs for pickup by the local dealers? Or is he just getting rid of the old stock that killed Samantha?

With my fingernails crying out in anguish I dig into the ground, gravel rising up to meet my palms, but I don't let the scratches stop me. This is it. This is my chance to prove to everyone that I haven't gone mad.

With a grunt, I pull the parcel from within its grave and drop it to the ground in front of me. With shaking hands I pull at the cord that binds its brown paper. Andrew has not taken much care to ensure the survival of the contents, I imagine it's due to be picked up sooner rather than later. If he actually cared about keeping it safe he would have wrapped it in plastic and gaffer tape.

The first thing I pull from inside its carcass is a photograph of Samantha. A recent one by the looks of her age. Time has not been kind to the girl that was briefly in my life, her cheeks are hollow and her eyes have sunk back, as though they've seen too much and want to escape.

The second item is a picture of Marcus and a receipt for a red handkerchief. I don't know what I expected when I followed Andrew out here, but it certainly wasn't a collection of trinkets.

The third item I place my hands on is a ring box. The same ring box I'd seen in Isabella's bedroom table. This is the ring Chris proposed to me with. This is my engagement ring. Why the hell did Andrew have this? What do I have to do with any of this?

I tip the parcel upside down, desperate to get this moment over with as part of my brain has already predicted what I'm going to find. The part of my memory that's shut itself down to protect me. I close my eyes and pick two items from the pile, I can't look at them, it's too painful. I can't think about it. I won't.

I managed to speak to a therapist once. By that, I mean one that I found rather than one the doctor recommended to me. They told me I was suffering from 'Dissociative Amnesia', that my brain had locked memories away from me to preserve itself at times of great trauma. They recommended I try Cognitive Behavioural Therapy or hypnosis to try and work my way through these blocks to learn healthier coping techniques.

Isabella had dismissed all of that though, and put me in touch with a 'legitimate' counsellor as she put it. They didn't agree with my original diagnosis. According to them the gaps in my memory were just due to common-as-muck depression and anxiety. The next therapist agreed. And the one after that until eventually

I'd forgotten about my original diagnosis.

But now I remember.

Now it's all flooding back to me.

Oh God.

I can hear an animal crying out in pain somewhere in the building site around me. I should go and check on it, and see if I can help. Then I realise that the noise is emanating from me. I'm the one howling in pain, in grief, in guilt and regret.

The moon is peaking out from beneath the clouds as I sit in the muck and grime I've dug up around me, surrounded by the belongings of dead people. Then, just as I've released all the horror from my body, something heavy hits the back of my head and the world turns black.

Chapter Twenty-One - Isabella

I wake with a start around 11 pm, my eyes flying open and staring into the darkness of my room. My breathing is rapid and I tell myself that whatever it was that's caused such panic was just a nightmare. It's not real. And yet my heart is thumping so loudly I can hear it in my ears.

Something isn't right.

There's a new air of chaos in my house. I can feel it.

Coldness nips at my feet as I push them out from inside the cosy cocoon of my bed. I won't be able to fall back to sleep until I've checked the house front to back.

Maybe I left the fridge door open? Or perhaps one of the windows is only just on the latch? Something has happened that pulled my subconscious from rest and I won't be happy until I've righted it.

I make my way down the stairs, avoiding the squeaky step so I don't disturb May. She deserves a good night's sleep before the events of the morning transpire.

I haven't quite made up my mind yet as to what I'm going to do but I have accepted the fact that I need to take action in the next twelve hours. I can't let this carry on any longer. It isn't fair to either of us.

With what I hope are soft steps I creep room to room, checking every power outlet and point of entry. This is a relatively safe neighbourhood but I probably should start acting with more care. The more waves I make in politics, the more pushback I can expect. It's not a complete stretch of the imagination to admit that one day I might find a stranger knocking on my door, mouth full of complaints at my voting decision on some matter or another.

To my relief, I had remembered to close the fridge before stumbling up to my bed. The online grocery shop had only just been delivered, and Andrew would be most put out to have to re-order anything outside of the agreed-upon schedule. Sometimes I worry that I've given too much control to my campaign manager, that he's responsible for too many corners of my life. Too many of my secrets. I need to start unpicking his webs, carving out independence from him.

Satisfied that I haven't left anything open or unplugged I make my way back up towards my bedroom. Hopefully my brain will let me sleep again. I need as much rest as possible to prepare for the morning.

The bathroom door has been left ajar, and I know I shut it behind me before I went to sleep. I always do. I guess May got up to brush her teeth sometime after I went to bed. That's a good sign at least, that she wants to take care of herself. Maybe there is hope that she'll recover without intervention.

Hope.

There's always bloody hope right before a fall.

Pills are scattered across the bathroom floor. Without drawing a breath I've turned on my heel and launched myself at May's bedroom door, praying she hasn't locked it.

I fall through its frame and am relieved to find the room empty. She hasn't taken her own life. She's still with me.

But where?

I turn a full three hundred and sixty degrees, scanning my surroundings, as though she's hiding somewhere and it's my job to find her.

I know she isn't downstairs. I painstakingly checked every inch of the rooms down there when I was certain I'd left something out of place.

She isn't in my room. I would have jumped out of my skin had she been and she isn't in the bathroom I've just come from.

Which means she's gone.

The reason for my sudden waking becomes apparent. The biological link between us alerting me, tugging me from sleep so I can problem-solve in the waking world.

My sister is missing.

There's no logical reason for her to be outside of this house at this time of night. I'm certain she isn't meeting a clandestine lover and the trains back to her town stopped running hours ago. Besides, no matter what was going on between us I know May would never head home without saying goodbye.

So that leaves me with two possibilities.

She left of her own accord under the guidance of her unwell mind.

Or she was taken.

But who would want to snatch May from my house? The only person she's irritated whilst being here is Andrew and I'm certain, hand-on-heart, that he wouldn't have kidnapped her. It's not his style. Still, my hand goes to the pocket of my dressing gown and reaches for my phone. I'll call him just to be sure.

Just to put my mind at ease.

The dial tone sets my teeth on edge and I find myself muttering pleas for him to answer until eventually the voicemail kicks in. Still, it's nothing to worry about, even Andrew sleeps occasionally.

Next, I scroll through my contacts list until I find James' number.

"Isabella?" he asks, his voice sounding groggy with sleep.

"James, I'm so sorry to wake you."

"It's not a problem. Is everything okay?" he asks.

"No. No, it's not. I've just woken up and May is gone."

He presses me for further details and relaying them thankfully slows my panic a little. James will take care of this. He will find my sister and bring her back to me. I can't have her wandering the streets doing and saying God knows what. Lord knows what would happen if she approached the wrong person.

"I'm scared she's going to hurt herself," I say, trusting him with my deepest fear. I've always tried to do right by May, always tried to protect her but the one thing I can't protect her from is herself.

"Stay put. I'll go out and look for her. She can't have gotten far." He says and after exchanging a few more reassurances we say goodbye.

It's hard to believe that James' only advice is to stay put.

I partially understand his reasoning behind it, if she returns it means I'll know straight away and be able to assess the situation first-hand. But can he really expect me to just sit here and do nothing when my sister is missing?

I pull an armchair across my living room, placing it in the bay of the largest window, and open the curtains. The world outside is dark and quiet and this does nothing to quell the growing worry that's taking up residence in every cell of my body.

Where is she?

What is she doing?

Who is she talking to?

No.

I mustn't let my mind go to the worst possible scenario. May is having a breakdown, yes, but there's still time for me to help her before it becomes too late.

Unless she's done something she can't come back from.

But that isn't like May. I have to keep reminding myself that not once has May ever been considered a danger to herself. She's never, ever, displayed suicidal tendencies. It's unlikely she'll start now.

Then I remember the pills spilt on my bathroom floor.

No.

There will be a logical explanation for those. If she were going to take an overdose she would have done it there and then. She wouldn't have taken herself off somewhere remote to die. She's not a dog.

Is that even a real fact? Or just something Marley and Me planted into my brain?

I pick up my phone and mindlessly scroll through Google to try and find the answer.

What am I doing?

I'm supposed to be waiting for May.

I put my phone face down on the windowsill, no more distractions, I need to be focused. I could miss her walking down the street past my house if I'm too busy in the world my mobile holds within its shiny screen.

My eyes are straining, trying to pick out her shape amongst the shadows, desperately hoping she's just gone for a late-night walk around the neighbourhood and soon she'll return. I don't want to blink too often in case that's the moment she makes herself known.

The text alert sound pings on my phone, breaking the silence I've cloaked myself in. My heart races as I see an unknown number appear on the screen.

There's no message of reassurance or explanation. Just a location pin. It must be a message from one of the burner phones she purchased.

She's still lucid enough to reach out to me for help, that's a good sign. If she were intending to do something stupid she wouldn't want me to be the one to find her, I'm sure of it. So the fact she's inviting me to join her must mean she's finally ready to ask for help.

I rush to the hallway and pull on the first pair of shoes I see, barely pausing to tie the laces of the trainers properly. They feel soggy under the soles of my feet. Of course they do, they're May's.

She probably wore them on the day James found her walking in the rain. Why didn't I make more of that moment? That should have been the red flag that alerted me to the fact she needed an intervention. But

I'd hoped it was just a blip.

Bloody hope.

Reaching up to the coat rack my hands instinctively go for my favourite red coat. Its warmth will be welcome tonight, but it comes up empty. She must have borrowed it on her way out.

I'll be sure to mention its significance to her when she's recovered. That coat was my mother's coat. The only thing of hers I'd willingly kept. I'm surprised May's never mentioned it. Then again I've built the kind of relationship between us where she wouldn't dare to bring that up. We don't talk about our parents. We barely talk about our pasts. All that matters is the here and now.

With a sigh I pull on my red macintosh and zip it up. Judging by the wind outside, a storm is on its way in and at least this option is waterproof. As I'm fastening up the buttons I call my usual town car service and am dismayed to find their offices unmanned. Next, I try a local taxi company, only to be told the wait is forty-five minutes for the next available car. I could walk to May's location in that time.

She's somewhere near my office block, that much I can tell from the pin. Finally I try James, if he's nearby I know he'll give me a lift - but my call goes to voicemail. He's probably too busy out hunting for May. To save him time I forward a screenshot of her message to him. There's nothing for it, I'm going to have to walk.

I'll be there in half an hour. Please wait for me.

I text May back on the unknown number, hoping that when the message is read my instructions will be followed. I can't have things getting out of hand - she needs to know that I am coming for her. That I'll be there for her.

Making sure to pick up my house keys before I leave, because I don't want to have to deal with calling a locksmith on top of finding my evasive sister, I shut the door behind me and set out towards May's location. Thankfully the route is mostly alongside a main road.

I give a brief thought to hitchhiking but there are two problems with this idea. The first being that I'll risk being recognised and gossip about my situation will spread and the second being the almost complete lack of traffic at this time of night.

Still, at least the wind howling around me hasn't yet turned into rain, and if I keep up a quick pace, I should make it to her before the storm breaks.

Chapter Twenty-Two - May

My hand rubs the back of my head as I wake up. What the hell happened?

I can feel a lump forming at the base of my skull and I wince as my fingers find it. Pulling my hand away I look around myself as I sit up. I'm in a lobby, although it's a stretch to use that word to describe my surroundings. Usually, when people think of a lobby, they think of a large welcoming area, the kind you'd find when you check into a hotel. This space was far from that.

There was a singular neon strip light just above my head. The bulb was fighting through its grimy enclosure as best it could. I admired its resilience.

The floor under my hands was sticky, and as I stood, I did my best to wipe the residue from my palms onto my coat. It left behind greasy prints, the kind caused by years of footfall and no care. Isabella was going to kill me when she saw them on her coat.

Isabella.

Just thinking her name causes a painful thud in my head.

The glass entryway door looks foreboding, thanks to the beam of streetlight that's filtering through its plastic covering. I dread to think about the germs on the handle as I push it down, ready to leave this place behind, but it doesn't budge. Again I push down, this time with more force, but the door will not open. I peer through the plastic but there's no one passing by that I can gain the attention of. Panic starts to tickle my throat.

Now I turn my attention to a wooden door just to my left. The number 6B is hanging precariously on its face.

It's a flat, I'm in a block of flats.

Knocking on the door I prepare myself for an angry tenant to come flying at me, it is after all far too late for a social call. But no such confrontation arises.

Pressing my ear to the door I knock again, hoping to hear some signs of life from inside, but there are none.

There's another door in this lobby and I repeat the process, but once again there's no sign of life. I look up towards the stairs in front of me. Surely if I just worked my way up the building I'd eventually find someone who could help let me out. There must be a trick to the front door, a certain way to jimmy the handle to get it to open .

From the state of the building, it wasn't well maintained so I imagine the tenants have had to put up and shut up with any issues with the main door. Landlords really can be the worst.

So I climb the stairs, knocking on each door, receiving no response. There isn't a sound in the air other than the ones I'm making. Something isn't right. There's no way every occupant in this block works night shifts. Someone has to be home.

By now I'm on the ninth floor and my breathing is becoming shallow, through exertion and nerves. I don't have the best cardio health of people, too addicted to my desk and the television to have paid it any mind previously. But now I desperately wish I'd at least gone for a jog once or twice in my adult life. Isabella would have no trouble handling this amount of stairs. Isabella never had any troubles at all.

My nerves are frayed by the time I knock on the last door, already knowing the response I'm going to receive. This time though, the door gives way slightly beneath my fist and it opens. There's a chain on the other side so I can't let myself in but at least I can peer through the gap.

"Hello?" I call, conscious that this could perhaps verge on breaking and entering. I can see an old-fashioned landline phone hanging on the wall, it's just out of reach.

"Hello?" I call again, as I push my body further through the gap. My armpit pinches against the door frame and the tendons in my wrist are screaming out at me to stop twisting them at such an unnatural angle.

The phone is only about an inch and a half away from my fingertips. If I can reach it then I can call for help, surely the police will understand my actions once they know I'm locked in an abandoned building.

Pressing my entire body weight against the door I pray for it to give. But it doesn't. It seems to be the one thing in this building that's actually been looked after, even the chain itself won't budge from the screws.

Now despair finds me and in a huff, I pull my arm back out into the corridor. I kick the door once in frustration, but all that achieves is to hurt my ankle. People kick doors down all the time, I've seen it so many times on television that it must be possible.

Writers wouldn't make that up. So I kick again, this time with my other foot but it's the same result. Just a sore sole and an overworked ankle.

I just need to reach that phone.

But I can't reach that phone.

The sound of a door shutting just above me grabs my attention. I cry out to it as I move up the stairs toward the final floor of the building.

"Hello? Can you help me?" I ask, but no one replies. Nevertheless, I keep climbing the stairs. Maybe this one singular inhabitant just didn't hear my plea. If I can catch up to them, then I can explain everything and they can help me get home.

In front of me is one singular fire door. The kind with the long metal bar in the middle that you press to open. As I place my hands on it I can hear the howl of the wind on the other side. At least this is some form of way out I suppose. And a fire exit is better than no exit at all.

I press down lightly on the bar, pausing, ready for the blast of the fire alarm, but it doesn't come. Unsurprising considering the state of the rest of the building. I feel for these tenants, I do. Their safety appears to hinge on the laziest of landlords.

Once I get home I'll be sure to report this building to the local authority. Somebody has to do something to improve things here. To force the landlord to act like a human being with empathy. What if there were a fire?

Nobody can get out the front door if they're in a hurry and the alarm system clearly isn't functioning. I don't want anybody's safety on my mind but my own, so I'll be sure to send a strongly worded email before I board my train home.

I don't even think I'll go back to Isabella's to get my stuff. If I do that, then I risk being carted off once again and I can't have that. Not now I know it's Andrew who's been causing my mental health crisis. I'm sure once I get home and convince my doctors to refill my prescription everything will start feeling better. If I see Isabella again before I manage to do that then my accusations will be chalked up as more paranoia, another reason to lock me away from the world.

No.

I have to take control of the situation for once in my life. I have to decide what's best for me. Not her. Never her.

The air outside the fire door wraps itself around me, invading the warm fabric of my coat until my skin is covered in goosebumps as its way of fighting back. Thankfully once I locate the emergency staircase I'll be able to get myself somewhere sheltered and warm. If I can find a nearby cafe I could even sit and have a hot drink whilst I plan my next move. God, that's a good idea.

I peer over the wall closest to me. No staircase down this side, but it's a hell of a drop.

I stumble slightly as I right myself, the knock to my head causing dizziness to come for me sooner than it normally would. Nausea begins to swim at the bottom of my stomach. It won't be long until it reaches my throat. Perhaps I'll put my fantasy of relaxing in a cafe after this on hold and take a trip to the local hospital instead. This seems like a head injury I should take seriously.

As I make my way towards the wall parallel to me I remember the sound of the closing door I'd heard back inside. The fire door had been closed tight, which means someone else must have come through it.

"Look," I start, "whatever it is you're doing out here, I won't tell anyone. I promise. I've no interest in anybody smoking anything or whatever it is. I just want to go home." I call out as the wind whips up my words and pushes them away from me.

Looking around though the roof seems fairly abandoned, there are a couple of air conditioning units which surprises me given we're in England, but other than that, there's nowhere else for someone to hide. Maybe coming out here was a mistake. The weather is beginning to kick up and my dizziness is growing worse with each minute. I should make my way back inside and sit down. At least then I won't be out here in the cold.

Eventually, someone will come home. If I make my way back down to the lobby I might even catch someone as they're heading in. Yes, that's a far better plan than trying to find an escape route that, let's face it, has probably rusted through given the state of the rest of the building.

But as I move back to the fire door, all hopes of a sensible decision evaporate. It's locked shut and you need a key to unlock it. A key that I don't have.

That's it. I've had enough of this.

Someone, some teenager or something, is out here on this roof and they must have a key to get back in. I've had enough of being ignored. They've heard me calling out to them, how could they not? And yet they've chosen to ignore me. That's just rude. And I'm sick and tired of people ignoring me.

"I've had enough now," I say as I march across the roof toward the air conditioning units, keeping an eye out for telltale smoke signals.

"You need to let me back into this building and out of the front door immediately." There's an edge to my voice that I haven't heard for many years. An edge that carries a warning. I am a woman on a mission. A woman who is strong and unyielding. A woman whom I thought I'd lost many years ago.

She's back now though. And I'm not about to let anyone chase her away again.

Rounding the side of the unit I expect to find someone cowering in my presence. Instead, I'm met with nothing. There is no one behind here. I have been talking to nobody but myself. There is no saviour on this roof with me. I am trapped and alone.

"May." Comes the one voice I'd desperately hoped not to hear. Because that voice, speaking my name, means that I'm in far more danger than concussion and hypothermia.

"Andrew," I reply, turning round to face him.

"I think we have a few things to discuss, don't you?" Andrew dangles a key out in front of me, the key to the fire door and most likely now I think about it, the front door.

This building is the block of flats I followed Andrew to.

This is where he's hidden his trophies for so long.

And now, I'm about to become one one of them.

Chapter Twenty-Three: Isabella

I'd spoken too soon because not ten minutes after leaving my house the sky began to drizzle. Pulling my hood tightly around my head I try to push through the wind to reach my destination.

I think I'm nearly halfway now but it's hard to be sure because of the lack of streetlights. Apparently, it's an energy-saving initiative to not have them all lit, really it's the council cutting corners so they can inflate their budget in other areas. That's something I'm going to address when I'm party leader.

Because I definitely am going to be party leader.

The notification for news alerts had sounded on my phone two minutes ago and I'd paused in my journey to take a look.

Numerous news outlets were running the photograph we'd leaked of my competitor - there's no way he'll recover from this in the public's eyes. At least not for a while. He'll be distrusted by them, and therefore by my peers, for a few months at least. And my party won't elect somebody they don't believe can win a general election.

That's where I come in.

Or at least I will if I can get this May situation under control.

With her in mind I pick up my pace, trying my best to ignore the arctic blasts of the storm on my face. My nose already feels numb and I know my cheeks will follow soon.

Why hasn't James called me back yet?

Surely by now he's checked his phone and got my message.

Knowing how diligent he is though, he's probably already on his way to the location I forwarded to him assuming that I'm still waiting at home patiently as he asked. I should have left him a voicemail and told him of my plan to reach her, why hadn't I done that? Because I was stressed. Because I was worrying about May. When I'm stressed I make rash decisions. Always have. Always will.

I wish I'd brought my wireless headphones with me, that way I'd have been able to call James without risking my phone getting soaked by the rain. Perhaps if I see a bus stop enroute I'll duck inside and give him a call. I'm sure he'll be happy to come and meet me, once he'd gotten over the fact I'd ignored his orders to stay at home and wait for an update.

Oh, and I need to call May's doctor as well. I need to advise him of the current turn of events so he can act accordingly. Now more than ever I know my options are thinning.

I had wanted to avoid another stay at the Sanctuary for her, but if it's the only way to keep her safe, then I have no other choice. To think that I had more options was foolish. It was hopeful and by now I should have realised that the world didn't run on hope.

I'd hoped I could trust Marcus with my private photographs.

I'd hoped I could trust Samantha to keep the past hidden.

I'd hoped Chris could fit into our lives rather than disrupt them.

I'd hoped my parents wouldn't turn into crushing disappointments.

Every single time in life that I've had hope the world has turned around and made a fool out of me.

Forcing me into situations I'd hoped would never transpire.

And now it was doing it again.

I'd hoped May wouldn't slip back into paranoia.

I'd hoped she'd be able to sleep it off.

I'd hoped her past would stay where it ought to.

But it had all started bubbling back up, memories she just can't keep locked away. Thoughts that cause her nothing but pain.

That's why she needs to get back into the Sanctuary. And this may be her longest stint there yet. I have to be absolutely sure, before she was released, that this time her mind was within her control. She didn't need to pick apart the things she'd forgotten. To do so would only cause her more pain.

It's why I'd demanded she stop seeing that quack who'd suggested hypnosis to help clear her dissociative amnesia.

I'd been so angry to hear her name her condition so fluently. For so many years I'd managed to keep it hidden from her under various doctors or therapists that I'd handpicked and this one, useless, individual had nearly torn all my hard work apart.

Any doctor worth a grain of salt knows that hypnosis shouldn't be used in the treatment of Dissasociative Amnesia because you run the risk of implanting false memories when you do so. I know that for a fact.

May can't know what she's forgotten.

She can't.

Because if she does then everything will change.

If she does the work and undertakes the therapy, then she'll remember. And I don't think she'd be able to cope with that.

I'd end up losing my sister. And I genuinely don't want that.

She might be a lot of work, and protecting her takes up more time than it ought to, but it's worth it because I owe May a lot. A lot more than she realises. There are debts between us that I can never hope to repay, so taking care of her, keeping her life easy and in order, is my way of making things right between us. All without her ever realising.

So yes.

I'd kicked right off when she told me about the therapist, their diagnosis and treatment plan. For a brief moment I had felt guilty about my reaction, because to her it must have seemed like it came out of nowhere, but to me it was the thing I'd been dreading since we were kids.

It's why when I sent May to the Sanctuary there were strict instructions that the professionals treating her must feed into the memory loss. They must make her believe that it's a normal and natural process. They should have taught her not to pick the scabs apart. Chris.

It had all been because of bloody Chris and his insistence that she seek independent advice. If he'd never done that, then I'm sure none of this would ever have happened.

He'd turned her into a ticking time bomb, and although it had taken years to come to fruition, now I was genuinely terrified she was about to explode.
I have done all of this for her own good. And she'll never see that.

By now I'm nearing my office building and I'm surprised to see that the streets are busier than I would have expected. Small waves of people are making their way down a side street to the left of my office, hurrying in their steps as though there is a party they're late for. I look around for May in the fast-growing crowds She'd told me she was here and therefore she had to be.

Ducking into a shop doorway I pull out my phone now safe from the rain's touch. Opening the message from her burner phone I zoom in on the pin she'd sent. It's not quite at my office, it's down to the left, towards
-

Oh no.
Oh no.
Towards the flat she followed Andrew to.
This is so much worse than I'd imagined. Running now I follow the swell of the crowd towards my destination, heart in my stomach at what I might find in front of me.

A pool of people have congregated on the street just outside the flats entryway. I push my way through them and hammer against the door, but no matter how much I try I can't get it to open.

"They've already tried that love," says an older man standing just off to the side of the crowd. "Emergency services are on their way to break it down."
Panting I give up my efforts to break into the building.

Now I look at the door properly I can see boot marks upon it, somebody - some good samaritan - has already tried to get in and failed. What hope do I have?

"Hey, aren't you..?" The man asks but I've moved away from him, losing myself in the crowd. Trying to see what they're all craning their necks at.

Then I see a flash of red amongst the dark sky.
May.
She's on the roof.

I scream her name, hoping it will carry itself up to her. Hoping that by noticing me I can stop the inevitable. But the sound doesn't reach her. It's whipped away by the wind that's only growing in ferocity.

"They think she might jump,"
"Nah, probably just wants attention,"

"People'll do anything for a bit of drama these days,"

I listen as people around me gossip about my sister. Trying to guess what the outcome of tonight will be. Their flippant behaviour towards her and what she's going through causes vomit to rise up my throat and I move away from them, hunching over some bushes until the heaving subsides.

My phone rings and I lift it up so I can see whose calling.

Andrew's name is on the screen and I watch until it rings off.

I'm not going to answer his call.

If I don't answer his call then none of this is actually happening.

If I don't answer the call then he can't talk to me.

Can't make me listen to him.

I look back behind me, up at the roof my sister has been spotted on. Now she's disappeared from view. Maybe this was all just to cause a fright, to make me see how much of a danger she was, how much danger she's in. Any minute now she'll come barrelling out of those doors and into my arms.

Any minute.

My eyes are laser focused on the front door although I know it's pointless.

Hope will once again make a fool of me tonight.

I'd hoped May could learn to cope.

I'd hoped she'd learnt to control herself and her memories.

I'd hoped we could grow old together.

But now I see that if it's come to this, down to this moment, that I can protect her no longer. She's too far gone. Too big a risk for me to manage any longer.

I can no longer keep my sister sane.

I can no longer keep her safe.

There is only one decision left to be made, and it's the one I'd hoped with all my heart I'd never have to make.

Hope, I think to myself with a twisted sad smile… Will be the death of me.

Chapter Twenty-Four: May

"I think we have a few things to discuss, don't you?" Andrew dangles a key out in front of me, the key to the fire door and most likely now I think about it, the front door.

For a moment, I think about snatching the key from Andrew's hand and making a run for it. But then he would know that I'm terrified. And I'm not about to let him know that. I still have my pride.

Plus, he'll easily outmanoeuvre me. He is closer to the door than I am right now and I know in a physical battle he'll surely win. It's obvious from his physique that he works out. If you add to that the fact he's already taken lives ,then it's clear my best bet right now is to keep him talking. If I can get him talking perhaps he'll become distracted and that will give me a chance to escape.

Andrew was a very smart man, but I was smart too. I had to hope he underestimated me.

"I suppose we do," I reply, gesturing to the floor in front of the air conditioning unit. It offered a little shelter from the wind and, to be honest, my head was beginning to throb so hard there was a chance I'd collapse if I kept standing. I wasn't about to make this too easy for him.

He smiled at me, like the snake in the Jungle Book, and I had to fight the shudder as it worked its way down my spine. Sitting down first I looked at the ground next to me, nodding my head in an invitation.

It was clear he thought he had already won by the way he followed my instructions quite willingly. I knew

Andrew would enjoy the theatre of this moment and it was my job, right now, to become the most captivated audience in the world. I had to stroke his ego to the point of explosion and hope that it caused a lapse in judgement.

"Have you discovered your pills?" he asks, leaning forward as he does so. The smell of the coffee on his breath turns my stomach and I shrug nonchalantly.

"Only this evening. Can't believe I didn't notice before then." I keep my tone light, as though we're just two friends sitting in the pub, talking about a well-mannered prank between us. It works because, as he smiles, I see a twinkle appear in his eyes. One that's pleased with my 'almost' praise. My plan might work. This could work.

"Ha! I did wonder when you'd spot them. Glad you did though, it's nice when art is appreciated."

So that's what he views this as? Art? Is that the way he viewed the deaths of Marcus? Of Samantha?

Of Chris?

Because Chris was dead. I can remember that now. The terror I'm feeling is tearing down the blocks my mind has put around certain memories. My brain is giving up on protecting itself because it can sense that the end is near. It isn't though. I won't let it be.

"What happened to Chris?" I ask, wanting to hear some semblance of the truth to help me make sense of the snatches of memories. I can remember blood. Chris' blood. It was everywhere.

"You truly can't remember, can you?" A look of sympathy briefly removes the self-satisfied smirk on his face. "Doesn't matter now, it was just the same thing that happened to the rest of them. Wrong person, wrong time."

"Because you love my sister?"

He stares at me in confusion. Perhaps he's never given a name to his feelings towards Isabella. Can obsession ever really be described as love?

"I don't love Isabella. I need Isabella. And she needs me. Together we are going to achieve great things."

"She doesn't need you," as soon as the words have left my mouth I know they are a mistake. Confusion is replaced by resentment on his face, I shouldn't have said that. I should have been smart enough to bite my tongue. I need to keep him calm and in control, if he's emotional then he's more liable to act rashly. More likely to be dangerous.

"You have no idea what you're talking about. You don't know what I've done for her. What I will do for her. I will do anything for your sister. I've told you that all along."

He isn't lying.

The one consistent trait Andrew has is that he will do anything to protect my sister.

It's just a shame that his mind is so warped he believes that killing others will protect her. When news of this breaks, the headlines will not be kind towards Isabella. She will be blamed in whispered conversations, her popularity will plummet and all of her dreams will turn to ash.

Maybe that isn't a bad thing.

Perhaps when she's free from politics she'll become more, I don't know, more human. Less controlling.

It's been the one driving force she's had since she was a teenager.

Most people her age had dreams of becoming pop superstars, streamers or artists. But not Isabella. Isabella wanted to be Prime Minister. She wanted the most important seat in the land. And nothing ever got in Isabella's way. Not even her own sister.

My hand is rummaging inside my coat pocket as I think about Isabella's incessant drive and of everything that those around her have been forced to sacrifice for her to achieve it. My fingers fidget with a chain, an item that fits naturally within the grooves of my fingertips, something I'd long forgotten about.

My plan to escape isn't going to work.

I know that deep down.

Andrew isn't going to let me leave.

I know too much.

And what I know will destroy Isabella.

He always protects my sister.

Always.

This will not be an exception.

"I saw that," he begins, "the fight leaving your mind. Acceptance of your fate taking its place. Pity. I'd hoped for more from you."

And he does pity me. I can read that in his eyes. This man, who holds my life in his hands, truly does pity me. I've never felt so small in my entire life.

"You know you don't have to do this," I say, knowing full well that he believes he does. With every fibre of his being, he believes that he has to kill me tonight, to stop me from exposing any secrets. I could promise him that I would disappear. That neither he nor my sister will ever see me again. That I'll never tell a living soul what I've worked out. But that would be a lie. And he's smarter than that.

"It's such a shame that you brought yourself up here. That you felt you had nowhere else to turn in life. If only there'd been more help, more support available to you then maybe you wouldn't have felt the need to throw yourself from the roof. Such an eloquent letter you left though. Printed on the best quality paper of course." He waves a folded piece of paper in my direction.

I listen to his words but they don't quite sink in. Not for a moment anyway.

Then all of a sudden my adrenaline kicks in. He's holding my suicide note. He's written me a suicide note. I jump up, despite my shaking legs, and run towards the fire door. I bang and bang on it with all my might, trying to make as much noise as possible. I'm hoping that somebody has finally come home. I scream until my throat is raw.

All the while Andrew stands off to the side, simply watching me.

I guess when your prey has nowhere to run then there's little point in exerting yourself trying to catch it.

I run to the side of the roof and wave at the people down below me, yelling out to them, but they either can't see me or hear me. The storm around us is swelling and I'm certain that I'm invisible to them through the rainfall.

Still, I just need one person to notice, one person to hear me, one person to save me.

There's a ringing sound on the roof and it stuns me.

A phone.

Andrew has his phone.

I lunge at him, nails drawn ready for battle, but it does me no good.

He has me pinned backwards, into his chest in an instant. One hand clamped around my arms and the other around my mouth. I try to shake him off, hoping to knock that stupid Bluetooth headset from his ears. If I can get the person on the other end of the call to hear me then maybe, just maybe they can help.

I can hear my sister's voice through the phone line and I want to call out to her, but his hand is clamped firmly over my mouth. I try to bite down into his palm but can't get a good grip on his flesh. She's asking to talk to me. He has to let her talk to me.

"I don't think that's the best idea," he replies and she goes silent. As though she's weighing up his response. As though this is a conversation they've had before. I know I'm not the most reliable sister. I know

I've caused her enough drama to last a lifetime but surely I deserve more fight from my flesh and blood. The silence down the line is crushing, and I concentrate on the ticking of Andrew's watch as my baby sister contemplates a way to talk this madman down from the edge. Think Isabella. Think. This man worships you. He will do anything you ask of him.

I can feel the very lip of the roof edge now underneath my feet, and I'm completely aware of the vast space of nothingness that lies in front of me. If I could call out to Isabella then I could tell her all of this. Tell her what words will save my life. Closing my eyes tightly I try to reach out to her, through some fabled biological link. To let her know that all she needs to do is ask him and he will obey. If she knew how much she meant to him then she'd understand. Then she could save me.

"Let her go, Andrew." She finally says. Four words and it's decided. She's done what she needed to do. She always does what she needs to do.

Andrew doesn't give her a response, he lets his arms drop backward towards the floor and I feel a sense of satisfaction wash over me. Finally, everything was going to be okay.

He turns me round to face him, pushes the note into my pocket and grabs me at the top of my arms.

"Like I said, I'd do anything for your sister."

And with that, he pushes me backwards.

Over the edge of the building.

And I'm falling.

And falling.

I can hear a woman screaming my name.

Isabella.

It's all clear to me now.

All the barriers in my mind shatter apart and I remember everything.

I clutch hold of the necklace in my pocket, of the ring at the tip of my finger as the world rushes towards me.

My parents were with me, even now.

Isabella.

She did this to me.

He was just obeying orders.

He was always just obeying orders.

Chapter Twenty-Five: Marcus

The wind was icy on Marcus' face as he walked back from the pub, thankful he'd sunk enough double vodkas and soda to keep the chill from his bones. Still, he made a point of pulling the top lapels of his jacket closer together in a show that he had respect for the weather.

Growing up his mother had always told him the story about the wind and the sun. How the two of them had been competing over who was the most powerful.

The wind had been boastful and egotistic, it would brag to the sun that it could force a jacket from a man walking nearby. It would be no trouble for its strong gales. But no matter how cruelly it whipped around the man his coat remained in place. The sun laughed at the wind's insolence and burst through the clouds, warming the air on the earth. The man smiled and removed his coat. The sun had won.

The lesson he had been supposed to learn from that fable had been to be kind. That he would get further in life behaving like the sun than the wind, that it paid to make others happy.

He'd always preferred the underdog, though, and was certain that if the wind had just been a little smarter, a little more creative, then it would have won the bet. After all, a tornado is just wind on a grand scale, and nothing outlasts a tornado.

That's how Marcus lived his life, as a tornado that crashed and tore through people, a short-lived power that changed lives as he saw fit. If his mother were still alive perhaps she'd eventually feel some sense of pride at her wayward son's success in life. True, that success had waned in recent years but he was certain he'd be on the up again soon.

All he needed was the payout from the papers for his photos of Isabella. And he could make some more measured investments, and if he could then resist the urge to get swept up with insider trading tips that never came to fruition, he'd be back on his feet in no time.

He supposed he should feel some level of guilt at selling the story of his relationship with Isabella, especially considering how many years he'd ignored the calls from journalists trying to buy his 'kiss and tell.' He always considered himself better than that, better than the tarts he and his friends scoffed at when headlines broke. But at the end of the day he had a choice to make - the life he wanted or the life he currently had.

He missed the designer clothes and cars, the expensive bottles of spirits in his kitchen consumed as an everyday beverage. He was a month behind on his mortgage payments and his penthouse apartment was the one thing he wasn't willing to lose.

The day the letter came from the bank to warn him of a foreclosure was the day he called the help desk of a national newspaper. The temporary blow to his ego was worth it when they agreed straight away to his fee - £250,000 for a two page interview and a 'never before seen' photograph of Isabella.

"I'm not a bad guy," thought Marcus to himself as he pushed his way through the dark night back towards his apartment. This time next week he'd be front page news. His bank balance would be restored, and it would be worth the ribbing from his friends.

He was on his way home to pick a photograph from his collection of exes and complete the questions the journalist had just emailed across. He'd be sure to choose a flattering photo of Isabella. He wasn't a monster after all. Perhaps the one he had of her lying in bed post coital, he'd snapped it when she wasn't aware ,and as far as he could remember, all her most important private parts were covered by the sheet. Well, barely.

A loud bang interrupted his train of thought, and he turned to locate its owner. It had sounded as though someone had dropped something large, and if it were an attractive young woman he'd be sure to offer his assistance.

He had never been able to resist a damsel in distress, and that had been the reason why his relationship with Isabella could never have lasted. She hadn't needed saving. She was too self sufficient, too career oriented - she wouldn't be happy to just stay at home and keep herself attractive. Marcus wanted to marry a trophy wife, not to become one.

Looking around into the darkness of the street he cursed the penny pinching council who insisted on only powering every third street lamp on this stretch of his walk. It meant he couldn't be certain if the noise had just been the wind knocking someone's bin over or if he should be on alert.

Reaching into his front pocket Marcus placed his fingers around his phone, remembering the anticipation he'd felt after his call with the journalist just before he'd arrived at the pub to celebrate. The hope it had ignited in him. Turning back towards the path that led to his home he pulled the phone out, wanting to call a friend, any friend, just somebody to talk to as the night grew darker.

Before he had the chance to decide on an acquaintance who would pick up at this time of night, or even unlock his phone to review his contact list, he found his face approaching the pavement at a rapid speed.

At the last minute, just before his nose connected with cement he found himself flipped over by the scruff of his neck. The back of his head snapped as it bounced to a stop on the floor and he heard a distinct snap on impact and he couldn't help the cry of pain that slipped from his throat. The sound of it though was soon snatched away as fear grasped hold of his throat preventing even air passing from his mouth.

In front of him stood a shadow dangling a cheese wire from its fingertips. It was impossible to make out any distinctive features from the nightmare before him thanks to the jet black mask they wore alongside the dark duster coat. Two heavy black boots winked at him in the moonlight. Marcus knew then, without a doubt, that this wasn't a casual mugging.

Whoever this was meant business.

"I can give you money," gasped Marcus as he went to sit up. The dizziness hit him worse than the boot that connected with his ribs in response to his offer. He could feel damp at the back of his head and yet, unusually, it hadn't rained in a couple of days. Vomit rose up in his throat and his vision began to drop out of focus. This head injury was serious. He needed urgent medical attention and unless he managed to sweet talk the figure in front of him, that wouldn't be possible.

"Please, I can give you whatever you want. Just let me call an ambulance." His breaths were coming out rapidly and he felt as though his heart were trying to flee the situation - so this is what real panic feels like. He thought he'd felt it before, on the day he received the call about his investments going bust, but now he knew that had been despair. This was true fear in all its gut-wrenching glory.

"My phone is in my pocket, please." He rasped through breaths he'd managed to steal from his lungs. The figure let the cheese wire dangle down towards the pavement as they knelt down and fumbled in his front pocket, going immediately for the right hand side. He supposed many people carried their phones on that side.

He watched as they pulled it to their face and tapped the screen. The ghostly light only served to highlight the loose threads in the balaclava, he couldn't even make out the eyes of his assailant due to the tinted glasses they wore.

He drew in a breath as the figure dropped themselves down onto his chest. They straddled him and he felt strong thighs squeeze against his ribs. The light from the phone screen blinded him momentarily as he looked into it, of course, he had Face ID enabled on his phone - the person on top of him couldn't unlock it without him. Obeying a wordless order he stared down the camera lens until he heard the unlock noise.

"Thank you," he whispered as they turned the phone back towards them. Perhaps they didn't know that you could call the emergency services without unlocking a phone, not everybody had the same model after all and he did pride himself on always having top level kit.

Rather than hearing a dial tone though, he could make out the typing sound of his keyboard as the person sitting on top of him wrote a message. He'd been told time and time again how obnoxious it was to keep that setting turned on but he hadn't cared until now.

He'd never cared about other people's opinions or comfort. He'd gleefully ignored all the resentful glances he'd received on public transport or in meetings as he typed out messages to friends or dates. But now the noise set his teeth on edge. Now he finally understood.

"What are you doing?" he asked and in response a hand clamped itself around his mouth. Woollen fibres embedded themselves onto his tongue as he tried to fight against the glove's grasp but it was no use. Even his arms wouldn't obey him anymore - it was as though his brain was slowly unplugging each of his limbs to ensure it could keep running.

He listened to the message sent tone as words that weren't his were sent to someone he didn't know. What exactly was this person playing at? Why didn't they just take his phone and run. It was worth at least eight hundred pounds and he'd never bothered to complete the insurance form on it so the IMEI number wasn't recorded anywhere.

He'd gladly give up his latest gadget if it meant this person would just stand up and leave. Their weight was beginning to crush his lungs and he had the feeling that they were slowly increasing the pressure with each second.

He watched as his phone was tossed to the side as the useless brick it was to his salvation. With a detached curiosity he watched as the gloved hand was removed from his mouth, taking in the shape of the hand he was sure would be forever imprinted on his face. He took the chance to call out and received a swift punch to his nose. The shock from the pain distracted him from the dull ache spreading from the back of his head and he tasted blood as it spurted from his nostrils covering his face and dripping down into his mouth.

He was incapable of escaping its flow and had no choice but to lie there, tasting his own mortality as the cheese wire was stretched out between the two gloved hands.

Although he had no way of knowing for sure he had a feeling that beneath the balaclava there would be a smile staring back at him. A large twisted one, like the Cheshire cat who got the cream. With a gentleness he hadn't been expecting the figure leant forwards towards him, the shift in their weight caused him to wheeze. The stale smell of coffee managed to seep through the threads of the mask and he wished with every fibre of his being that he could scoot back away from it. He was certain if he tried hard enough he could guess what blend had been the choice of the person about to kill him.

Because that's where this was going.
Marcus knew that now.

He wasn't meant to survive this encounter.

Everything about it had been planned. His face had been saved from the pavement because whoever now held his life in their hands hadn't wanted to take the chance it would prevent his phone from recognising his face and unlocking. They had needed to send that message. That's what this had all been about.

As the wire pressed against his neck he felt a momentary sense of calm. At least it would be over soon. The pain in his head would be nothing but a distant memory and the throbbing of his broken nose would be a thing of the past. At least soon it would end.

They say that when you're seconds from death your life passes before your eyes - but that didn't happen to Marcus. He wasn't able to tear his eyes away from the horror sitting on his chest and as the wire cut his artery and blood sped from his neck he felt something being stuffed into his mouth. But he didn't care, because he wasn't here anymore.

Somewhere on the other side of town a journalist's phone beeped with an incoming message.

I've changed my mind - Marcus.

Chapter Twenty-Six: Samantha

Samantha leant back in her desk chair and stared at her computer screen. The two words, written in large font, brought her a sense of relief.

The End.

She'd spent so many weeks working on the manuscript of her autobiography that she thought she'd never reach this point. But here it was. She was finished.

Well, not quite. She still had to find someone to edit it for her and then work out how to upload it to the storefront, but at least for tonight she could draw a line underneath this project and tell herself she'd done a good job. It had been hard at times to keep pushing on with the writing process, especially when the press and general public didn't seem quite as interested in the laundry she had to air than she was expecting. She'd hoped that by now she'd have been invited onto at least a couple of local news channels to gossip about Isabella and the truth that Samantha had been touting she was about to spill.

That would come though. She knew as soon as the book was in the public domain, interest would just grow and grow. There was no way it couldn't after she showed the nation just how sadistic their sweetheart had been as they grew up together.

She took a selfie with her screen in the background showing those two words and posted it online with the caption:

#Finallyfinished

It didn't take long for the trickle of messages and reactions to begin. The press may have no interest in her story, but all sorts of long forgotten friends were suddenly desperate to reconnect. They either asked her outright if they were featured in the book or beat around the bush for a few days before making a gentle enquiry.

She never responded to that question though - she relished the power it gave her over people. She imagined them squirming in their seats as they checked their phones repeatedly, waiting for her to write back and settle their nerves. If there was one thing in life that Samantha craved more than fame and attention, then it was power. And threatening to be honest about one's past gave you a hell of a lot of that.

The only people from her earlier years that she had purposefully excluded from the pages were those from her recovery support group. If it hadn't been for them, then she would have died from an overdose many years ago and so she kept their secrets to herself. She counted that decision as good karma to outweigh the bad that dredging up the past would bring her.

She knew that by inviting people into her life like this, less-than-flattering stories would be made known about her. Her criminal record would be aired. True it was light, and hadn't been made use of since she served her twelve-month sentence for burglary, but it was still there, and Isabella's team was sure to leak details of it to the press. But she wasn't afraid of Isabella. Not anymore. That's the only upside of having sunk to the levels she had when in the grips of addition. Very little frightened her anymore.

Back when she knew Isabella, or Izzy as she'd wanted to be known when she was young, it had been a different story entirely. Izzy had frightened her, more often than not, with her tenacity to always get her own way.

They'd been two teenage girls and as was always the case in those situations, one had been the leader and in their case that had always been Izzy. She decided who they sat with at lunch, what lessons they skipped, and which of the other girls they picked on. Izzy was the queen bee and, truth-be-told, Sam had always been happy to follow.

Their friendship had been deeply intense. The first time they met had been in the toilets at school. Sam had been hiding in a cubicle to avoid a lecture from her teacher on her late homework and Izzy had been sitting on a sink smoking a cigarette.

The smell had caught Sam's attention and slowly she'd pulled the door open a touch, peering out to see who was standing there, and what her chances were of bumming a smoke. Fortunately for her Izzy had offered her the pack without a single word having to pass between them. From that moment on they had been inseparable.

Together they took over their small corner of the school and ruled it with an iron fist. Samantha had started drinking regularly during that time, always happy to finish the shots that Izzy left to languish on the bars at house parties. Looking back she knew it was her first attempt at blocking out guilt with a substance over the daily bullying the two of them dished out, but at the time, she'd just assumed she was more of a party girl than her friend.

And that assumption is what Izzy exploited when she came home from a sleepover smelling of vodka and cigarettes. It had been Samantha, she'd told her parents through crocodile tears. She'd just gone along with her to the party to keep her friend safe. Izzy was a good girl.

A kind girl. And no matter how much they wanted their golden girl to break apart her friendship with Samantha, she never listened.

Until that one night.

Even now, over twenty years later, the memories of that night and what they did to that girl causes her hand to ache for a drink or something to smoke. True her recollections of the incident were slightly hazy but she was sure of one thing - it had all been Izzy's fault. The subsequent cover up may have been more of a split affair but Samantha definitely hadn't been the master mind.

She still wrote letters of apologies to the girl, or victim as her therapist had encouraged her to name her, but had never had the stones to post one to her family. To do so would dig up too much pain for them, and land her in a heap of hot water without any benefits. At least by telling the story in her own words she could control the narrative. She could paint a clear picture, one in which Isabella was the true monster and she was a naive follower.

Samantha had finally found an employer who didn't care about her criminal record, nor her past substance abuse - provided she consented to regular drug tests. Which she happily did whilst inside she seethed. No matter what she did in life she would never be trusted.

This new employer was no different. She very much doubted that every employee on their payroll was subjected to random testing. Despite telling her how proud they were of her and what a survivor she was, they were still judging her. Waiting for her to fail. It had happened to her time and time again. Eventually Samantha would tire of their hypocrisy and quit. She always did. This book was her only chance at a regular income.

Isabella was popular though.

Isabella wasn't struggling for money or employment. The country basked under her sunlight while Samantha was left to wither in the shadows. It wasn't fair and that's where the idea of the autobiography came from. On the surface she'd been marketing it as a 'survivor's story' - people loved those. A tale of a woman who went to the very brink but pulled herself up by her bootstraps and turned her life around.

But beneath that veneer lay the real story, a chance to see the real side of the country's most popular politician. True, no agent had wanted to touch her manuscript, and pre-orders were non-existent, but she knew that when word got out about her book's content, copies would fly off the metaphorical shelves.

A smile crept onto Samantha's face as she stretched her arms above her head, imagining how Isabella would react when she hit the publish button. That bitch hadn't bothered with her since the day her parents finally ended their friendship, but now she'd have to pay attention. Now she'd have to acknowledge the friendship they shared and the mistakes they made.

Mistakes.

That was a light way of putting it.

They hadn't meant for the girl to fall. That's what Isabella had said as they looked over the edge of the derelict pier. They were just supposed to scare her a little, challenge her to be as daring as they were, put her in her place. But Isabella and Samantha were familiar with every plank of that pier, they knew where the rot had set in on the safety rails. Kayla didn't.

Samantha's back had been turned when she heard the crack and she'd whipped around to find Isabella with her arms outstretched towards the tide. The rail that Kayla had been standing next to was long gone.

"What have you done?" asked Samantha.

"What have we done?" Isabella replied.

Snapping herself back to the present Samantha finally stood up from her desk. It had been a very long day and tomorrow she had to work out how to format and upload the damn thing. She should get an early night so her brain was fresh. A quick cup of tea, twenty minutes in front of the television, and then bed. That seemed sensible.

Standing up she heard her knees crack and once again cursed her past self for living so thoughtlessly. She bet Isabella's joints didn't creak and groan. They probably sang a lullaby as she floated through life.

Some had accused Samantha of being the green-eyed monster when she'd first started promoting her book in online forums, and despite how she openly protested, deep down she knew there was an ounce of truth.

A loud ringing interrupted her jealous thoughts and her eyes swung to the clock. It was 10 p.m. Who on Earth would be ringing her doorbell at 10 p.m? Instantly her mind raced to the worst-case scenario - it was the police who had come to inform her that her mother had been in an accident. The two of them had only just reconnected after years of bad blood between them, which had been solely Samantha's fault, so the idea of losing her now was Samantha's biggest fear.

With this in mind, she picked up her step as she moved towards the front door, nervous hand turning the lock, tears already brimming in her eyes.

But nobody was there.

The front step was empty. The only sign that she hadn't imagined the doorbell ringing was the motion-sensitive light that was coming from the porch.

"Bloody kids," she muttered to herself as she pushed the door closed and turned the lock. Shaking her head slightly she walked back down her hall towards the kitchen and switched the kettle on. She watched the side panel on it as the water began to bubble, it was therapeutic, like an out-of-control lava lamp.

A sharp prick at the back of her arm broke her out of her trance. Whirling round she was shocked to find a figure covered head to toe in black standing just behind her, the back door to her kitchen wide open. Looking down she noticed the needle in their hand and gasped.

"Who the fuck are you?" she panicked, her hands grasping behind her on the counter, desperately searching for the knife block. The figure didn't reply. They didn't move. It was as though she hadn't even spoken.

The world was beginning to grow soft around the edges and Samantha felt the familiar warmth spreading through her veins - heroin. They'd injected her with the drug she'd fought so hard to stay clean from.

Her hand finally found what she had been looking for and she pulled one of the knives from the block, never letting her eyes leave the person in front of her. Her limbs were growing heavy though, welcoming back their old friend with open arms.

She stumbled as she tried to take a step towards the intruder, waving the knife around like a flag at a coronation parade. They stepped forward and grabbed her arm, holding her steady. She was almost grateful for their support, until she felt the prick of a second needle enter her skin. No. That's too much. Stop.

Unsure if she'd spoken aloud or not Samantha had no choice but to allow the stranger to guide her steadily onto the floor. Until she was sat with her back against the kitchen cabinet.

They brushed a strand of hair from her face and she smiled at them through dreamy eyes despite the fear she felt. It would be so easy to float away right now.

A third prick of a needle and the world began to fade around Samantha.

The last thing she saw was a black shadow leaving her kitchen, carrying her laptop.

Chapter Twenty-Seven: Chris

"You don't have to do this you know," Chris says, trying to keep his tone from sounding too pleading. If they see him as weak then they'll rush the job. He has to keep them talking and engaged until someone gets home.

His hands are pulled together tighter in response behind the chair, but what did he really expect? A heart-to-heart?

No.

They were too far gone to pretend to see the other's point of view. All he had to do was stay alive for a little longer and help would come. Why did he start that argument? Why pick today of all days, and why wait until they were alone?

He should have taken them out for lunch, confronted them in public and let the pieces fall in a much more controlled environment.

Instead, he rushed ahead, wanting to act the moment he discovered the truth, fuelled by a sense of injustice. Just for once he should have bitten his tongue. But he was a passionate man. It's what had drawn May to him in the first place.

His paltry kicks as they tried to bind his feet only succeeded in knocking the chair he was bound to over onto the floor. His head hit the ground with a thud, luckily missing the lip of the marble counter by an inch.

"That would have been too easy," they sighed as they pushed him back into a sitting position. He couldn't tell if that was genuine remorse or sarcasm. He couldn't tell much about the person in front of him at all.

With two zips he was completely trapped, unable to even draw a deep breath thanks to the rope around his chest. He never should have accepted that drink. It was uncharacteristic for them to make him one. He should have known better especially given the bombshell he had just dropped into the room between them.

But he'd been foolish, too trusting despite all he knew. And to be honest, he needed the alcohol to help dull his rage. He wasn't a violent man and he hadn't intended to become one today, but he knew that if somehow he were able to escape he wouldn't stop punching until he felt brain beneath his fists.

For the first time, in a long time, he wished he wasn't estranged from his parents. At least then there would be someone to miss him should the worst happen this afternoon. And, despite his hopes for rescue, he had a feeling that he wouldn't be alive to see the sunset. Even if he managed to live, life would never be the same. Not for him and not for May.

"How could you do this?" he asks, moving his head out of the way of the gag they were trying to place across his mouth.

"I'm just doing what needs to be done."

"No. You're not. What needs to be done is you need to stop this. Stop all of this. Stop the lying, stop the violence and abuse and own up to what you've done."

They laughed at his suggestion, and stood before him motionless. A detached smile spread across their face. Chris had been in trouble before in his life - bar fights, being mugged, that one argument with his dad - but this was the first time he felt truly terrified. It felt like even his blood was screaming at him.

"That can't happen," they replied once they'd finished laughing. "I'm doing it for her."

This time it was his turn to scoff. That was the biggest lie he'd heard from their lips so far. None of this was for her, it was all for them. For what they wanted. To try and dress it up as a sacrifice on their part was insulting.

"May will never forgive you."

"May will never know."

"She'll know. She'll know I didn't just walk away and disappear. She knows how much I love her, how much she means to me."

A sharp punch was delivered to his nose, and the room spun momentarily.

"You know nothing about love," he spat, having given up on keeping his temper in check. He had very little to lose now.

"I know you don't hurt the ones you love. I know you don't drug them, manipulate them, lie to them, and fucking section them for your own convenience." Isabella looked stunned by his outburst. As though that thought had never occurred to her.

"I love my sister," she protested, her voice soft and lost.

"You love yourself more." Chris knew he was antagonising her, in the same way he knew the instant he confronted her with the truth that he wasn't going to walk away from their conversation alive. He couldn't help himself though. The second the envelope from the private investigator came through the mailbox he'd been vibrating with incandescent rage.

There had always been something not quite right about May's diagnosis. Something about her sister's overt involvement in her care that didn't sit right with him. And the envelope had confirmed all of his suspicions.

May's medical records proved that other than a touch of depression she didn't have a mental illness, she had dissociative amnesia. It had started the day their parents died. That's when gaps in her memory started appearing and the first reports of paranoid accusations were recorded. It all revolved around that night.

"What happened the night your parents died?" he asked.

With nothing to lose he decided to ask the question that had been itching at his brain since he discovered the truth. Isabella had used their inheritance to line the pockets of doctors willing to bend the rules, to tell the story she needed May to believe, a way to keep her big sister in line.

Isabella had been fifteen the night their parents died, and yet she showed a level of control and forward thinking that people twice her age didn't have a grasp on. It sickened him to think of how that skill must have aged alongside her.

How many strings was she pulling now? How many more pockets were lined so she could have her own way? His future sister in law was broken. Fundamentally twisted and broken. And now he was at her mercy.

"That's not your concern," she replied coolly, dropping the gag to the floor, having given up on using it. Or perhaps she was enjoying this conversation, of having someone truly seeing all of her. Whatever the reason Chris felt a glimmer of hope.

"You could just let me go and I'll disappear?" he suggested.

"You love my sister."

"I do."

"So I know you're lying."

"I am."

It had been a pointless attempt at escape, he knew she'd see through his lie the instant it was uttered, but he'd had to try.

Isabella moved over to the counter and began to finger the knife block, pulling each out and considering it. At least his death would be quick.

"You love your sister."

"I do."

"I know you aren't lying."

"I'm not." Finally happy with her choice she moved back towards him, blade in hand.

"Why do this to her?" he asked.

"It's the only way to keep her safe."

She was inching closer to him, soon the blade would be at his throat and it would be over.

"Why?"

"Because she knows too much," she replied, a sad look flickering across her face and he believed her. He now believed that she thought keeping May in the dark about her mental health was the right choice. It was safer, somehow, for May to believe she was just paranoid rather than on the money when it came to her suspicions about her sister.

"Who are you protecting her from?" he asked as the metal tip was pushed towards his throat.

"Me," Isabella replied as she slashed.

She stood over Chris' body as the blood seeped out of him, listening to his final death gurgles as he left this world for the next. Guilt was an emotion she didn't often trifle with but she did feel it in this moment. May had loved this man, truly loved him. And she'd just taken him away from her forever.

It was the only option though. It was that or have him reveal the truth to her sister.

And if May learnt the truth then she would seek the correct treatment.

She would remember about Samantha and the girl Isabella had pushed from the pier.

She would remember the night of their parents' accident.

She would remember too much.

And everything Isabella had worked so hard for would be taken away. All the things she had done, the palms she had greased, the favours she had bartered and the lives she had ruined would be for nothing.

And then Isabella would have to do the one thing she'd always swore not to do.

She'd have to kill her sister.

Chapter Twenty-Eight: Mum & Dad

Isabella stood staring out of the window, watching as her parents' brake lights disappeared into the night. She could hear the noise of her older sister, May, as she began clearing up the plates from dinner. With a sigh she decided it was time to confront her.

May was busy scraping leftover food into the bin from the plates left behind. Their mother had cooked them both dinner before she left for an evening out on the town with her husband and his business partners.

Dad on the other hand had spent most of his time fussing about how he looked and stealing worried glances at his youngest daughter. She wasn't going to run her mouth though. She had as much to lose as he did if the truth came out.

Isabella watched her sister as she busied herself playing house. She pitied May really, almost as much as she loved her. They had a somewhat complicated relationship, May was always trying to parent her. She'd been that way since Isabella was eleven - since the night with Samantha and Kayla on the Pier.

Her parents' treatment of her had changed that night and May desperately tried to fill the void they'd left behind. It wasn't that her mum and dad no longer loved her. They still cared for her, still made sure she had everything she needed, but for the last four years they'd made it clear that they no longer truly liked her.

That they feared her. That they would fulfil their parental duties but nothing more.

There were no more movie nights, shared secrets or inside jokes between the three of them. Where once she'd been confident that she was the golden child, the chosen one, now she was sure she'd tumbled below even the postman in their estimations. He at least got to partake in small talk with the two of them each morning.

Her parents no longer hung on her every word and story. They merely nodded where necessary and moved onto their next task as quickly as possible.

May had stepped in where they'd stepped back. It was she who helped Isabella with her homework, who took an interest in the playground gossip as they brushed their teeth together each night and it was May she turned to with all her troubles and fears. May had slowly become the mother Isabella had all but lost and it was thanks to her older sister's guidance she'd taken an interest in politics, making the decision to run for a spot on school council in her final year. The two of them had even stayed up late last night discussing ideas for her campaign.

So it was a shame she had to have this conversation with her, because she was worried about how it might end.

"May, do you help dad with the accounts?" Isabella asked, stepping over the door boundary into the kitchen.

"No, he's never let me look at the books. I mostly just book appointments," May replies, having finally scraped all the leftover food from the plate. She turned on the tap and squirted some washing up liquid into the bowl. There was something about cleaning that she felt calming, and she never minded doing Isabella's chores as well as her own.

May has been working part-time in their parent's company for the last six months, hoping to save up enough money to go travelling. Isabella knows she would never actually go though. Her sister was no longer the go-getting socialite she used to be. She might think she's hiding her growing social anxiety well but she's not. Not to the one person who knows her best in the world.

"So you didn't know he's been embezzling money?" Isabella's question is forthright and abrupt, she sees little point in beating around the bush. Not when the answer is so important.

Because if May knew that would leave Isabella with an impossible decision. Could she trust her sister to keep their father's secret? Could she rely on May that deeply? And if she couldn't, how would she handle it?

She'd been spitting feathers when she'd found the anomaly in the businesses bank statements. Poking around in her father's office often led to dirty secrets about others being exposed to her gain, but that day she'd come across one she would have to guard for the rest of her life.

If the truth came out and her father was charged she would be tarred by his crimes for the rest of her life. People at school would avoid her in corridors, that's if they could even afford to stay in their neighbourhood. They'd probably lose their home in the process of his legal battle.

There would be a new school, a new hierarchy to uncover, and a never ending sea of whispers following her room to room. She'd be the thief's daughter.

Forever the first to catch blame should anything go missing - the apple doesn't fall from the tree is what they'd say.

Whenever she started a new job they'd see her surname and the address of the school where she gained her qualifications and join the dots. Nobody wants to hire the child of a criminal, that's just inviting trouble to your door.

And she certainly couldn't pursue a career in politics, which was her dream. Every byline about her would at least allude to her father's embezzlements, she'd be just the same as every other politician in the public's eyes - crooked.

Isabella wanted to change the country. To bring good to every home. She was the only person who was capable of doing that. The only one strong and honest enough. And she could only do that if she succeeded in her career, if she became Prime Minister and took responsibility for everyone.

That would never happen if the truth came out.

When she confronted her dad, at first he'd tried to spin the situation around. Telling her that he was the one with the right to be furious because of her snooping.

Next came the denial, "how could you believe me capable of that?" he'd asked.

And finally the acceptance, the apologies and the promises to do better.

Isabella had watched him cancel the regular payments that were set up between the business account and his private one, the one made to look like a direct debit to a legal firm, and she was certain the matter was dealt with.

Until her dad received an email from his business partner.

He'd wanted to meet up to discuss some anomalies he'd noticed. The man was an accountant by trade, a useful skill to have in a business partner, but not when the business was undertaking illegal transfers.

She convinced her dad to put the meeting off. They came up with excuses together. Each time she had a demand her father would agree, she could see his fear of her grow everyday - and she relished in it.

He actually tried to convince her that he'd stolen the money for them, for his family. It was probably the biggest lie Isabella had heard in her short time on the Earth.

He'd done it for himself.

Because he wasn't happy with what he had. Because he wanted a lifestyle that was out of his reach. They didn't need expensive holidays twice a year or the latest tech. Sure it was all enjoyable, but not needed. He was the one who wanted to keep up appearances in certain circles. If he'd done it for them then he would have put the girls into private education rather than buying himself the latest Mercedes. She'd bitten her tongue though. Her father had to believe that she'd forgiven him. That he'd absolved himself when he stopped stealing. That was the only way her plan was going to work.

May was staring at her, plate hanging from one hand and dishcloth from another. Isabella could tell from her expression that this was news to her and she sighed with relief.

At least her sister was still as honest as she expected her to be.

Now she just had to make sure May kept their family's secret. Briefly Isabella berated herself for confronting May. If she'd just kept her mouth shut then her parents' crimes would have died with her. But she'd had to know if May was innocent. She couldn't have such impulsive people in her life. They weren't worth the risk to her reputation.

"What do you mean?" May asked.

"Dad's been skimming money from the company. Mum's the secondary signature on the transactions." Isabella replied, needing her sister to feel the weight of their parent's failures. When she'd first discovered the transactions she'd desperately hoped her mother was as clueless about them as she was, but with a few clicks of the mouse, she learnt that not only did her mother know about the money - that she'd played a key role in stealing it.

"Fuck." May didn't swear often, so Isabella knew she was floored by the news. "Does anyone else know?" she asked.

"I think Roy knows," answered Isabella, keeping her response vague despite knowing this for certain.

"What? But he was completely normal when they were just here. How could he sit across from them after that?"

The truth was Roy had no choice but to conduct himself as normal. He was being blackmailed to do so - by Isabella over a lovechild his wife wasn't aware of. People were just such a letdown.

"I don't know. Maybe they paid him off?" Isabella suggested without the slightest flinch at her lie.

"What do we do?"

"We can't tell anyone, May."

This was the crucial point in their exchange. If May stepped out of line, then it would be the end of their relationship. If she couldn't see how important staying quiet was, then Isabella would have to remind her.

"No, I know. But, like, what do we do?" May asked.

Isabella couldn't fight the smile that appeared on her face. Of course she could trust May to see the bigger picture. She could always rely on her big sister.

"Dunno. I guess we just hope karma doesn't bite him in the ass."

Isabella turned her back and went to head into the living room. The conversation had served its purpose and now all there was to do was wait.

The sound of sirens began to swell in the distance and she stood motionless at the living room window as the night sky began to awaken with flashing blue lights.

After about twenty minutes May came to stand next to her.

"What do you think happened?" she asked as the phone began to ring.

"Karma," replied Isabella.

Twenty years later, as May felt the air shift around her as it tried to compensate for her presence, she looked back on that night, wondering why she didn't see the signs, or rather why she chose to ignore them.

It had been right there, in front of her face and deep down she'd known what her sister had done. She knew that her sister had killed their parents.

She'd known it the moment Isabella had stood to watch the emergency response from their living room window. Such detached pleasure she seemed to take in the drama growing around them.

At the funeral the truth had bubbled away inside of her as she listened to their parents' eulogies. She took in sympathetic words from the congregation, all while Isabella sat next to her staring blankly at their coffins. Coffins she had put them in.

The rage she felt in that moment came to her again now, except now, as she fell towards the pavement the rage was aimed at herself. She should have done something about Isabella back then. She could have saved so many lives if she hadn't been blinded by her love for her younger sister. If she hadn't let her control her life and send her for brainwashing sessions at the Sanctuary.

Because that's all it had been.

Isabella had been controlling May's life since she murdered their parents and it could only ever have ended this way for her. She could never outlive her sister's ego and bloodlust.

May's last thought, before peace swept over her, was that at least now she would be free of Isabella. She would be somewhere she could no longer hurt her. She could be with her parents, be with Chris and finally, finally be allowed to be happy.

Chapter Twenty-Nine: Isabella

"Let me talk to her, please."

I cradle the phone between my chin and my shoulder as I walk towards the building where I know Andrew will be waiting. Somewhere up there in the skyline my sister is waiting, waiting for me to say the right thing to Andrew and save her life.

"I don't think that's the best idea," he replies and he's right. If I speak to her I'm bound to say the wrong thing, to give her words that are better kept in my head, to say I'm sorry about tonight. About so many things.

"Let her go Andrew."

Four words and it's decided. I've done what I needed to do. I always do what I need to do.

I watch my sister float through the air, like a gravity defying ballerina and I'm stuck for a second in my feelings towards her.

I don't often have regrets about the decisions I have to make, but I feel like this one may live with me for a while.

The street around me lights up with phone camera flashlights which only highlight her descent towards us. I can see the red of her coat, my coat, as though it's a warning beacon. Telling me that this time I've gone too far. That killing May is a decision I can never come back from.

My jaw is aching and it's only then that I realise I'm screaming. It's as though I'm a banshee finally horrified by my own actions.

Chris, Samantha, Marcus, Agatha, Mum, Dad - none of them had this effect on me. All of them had deserved their fate, all of them had threatened my future but not May.

May had always, always supported me. Always believed that I would achieve great and life changing things. Her one mistake had been remembering all that I'd done. If she'd just left well alone, if she'd never come to stay with me, then she never would have found that drawer. Never would have grown suspicious, or followed Andrew. And she would have never found the trophies he was burying for me.

Why did you have to do that, May?

Why did you have to leave me no choice?

On autopilot I find myself moving towards the end of her path, where an abandoned car waits unsuspectingly in a parking bay. I need time to stop, to slow, I need to catch her before I lose her. Her screams are beginning to come into focus now as she approaches her finale and I know they will haunt me for the rest of my nights.

I scream out her name, hoping it will carry up through the air towards her. That she'll hear it, and in her last few moments, forgive me.

Two strong arms wrap themselves around my waist and I'm hoisted slightly above the payment so my feet can no longer carry me towards my kin. I thrash around as best I can, but it's no use. My sister lands on the roof of the car with a noise so horrific it causes a collective gasp from everyone around us. It felt like a small bomb exploding as the metal twisted to give life to her form. The car sighs in defeat as glass shards shatter into the world around us.

I scream her name over and over, hoping it will wake her up. That she'll sit up and dust herself off and the two of us can talk about all that has led to the moment.

She'll understand eventually. I know she will. May always understood me. Always stood by me, even if she can't remember it.

The arms around my waist loosen and I break free. Under different circumstances I'd be proud of the show I was putting on for the multiple witnesses, whose attention was now all turned towards the wailing woman I'd become, but this wasn't for show. Not yet anyway. This was real, perhaps some of the first real emotions I'd had in a very long time. My big sister was gone and I was finally all alone in the world.

There's a wall of emergency service workers between me and May and I yell at them that I'm family but they don't let me pass. I go so far as to ask them if they know who I am but they just offer me sympathetic expressions and platitudes as they tell me she's gone. That she died on impact with no hope of survival. That I'm best not to look, that I wouldn't want to remember her in this way.

A friendly paramedic leads me towards a waiting ambulance, gently placing their arm around my shoulder. Usually I would shrug this level of familiarity off but right now I'm too numb to be incised. I'm offered a foil blanket as though that could solve all my problems, as though that could undo what I've just done. I take it though, it can't make this situation any worse.

Then I hear his voice and I realise perhaps I'm not totally without family, maybe I can someday start a new family. One that I'll protect with my life.

"I'm so sorry for your loss," James offers. A phrase I'd gotten used to at my parents' funeral. I wonder if I'll feel a pang of guilt every time I hear about May?

I didn't at mum and dads funeral. But I suppose that had been different circumstances. Their deaths had been justified to serve the greater good. May's was not.

May's was a selfish snap decision I made - the easy way out - and I'll always wonder if I could have approached the problem she presented differently.

All I can do is nod my head at him. A way to acknowledge his sentiment without conversing about it. I don't think I could find the words right now. The paramedic is right, I am suffering from shock. As a chill creeps up my spine I pull the foil blanket closer around myself, grateful now for its presence.

My sister is dead.

My sister has died.

And it is all my fault.

I shouldn't have reacted so quickly. I could have tried to reason with her after Andrew discovered she'd been following him. I know I would have been able to talk her round. For so many years now all I've thought about is my future. How to protect it and how to achieve it. And never, not once did I consider that May wouldn't be in it.

"Thank you," I whisper to him and I feel the switch in my brain click into place. My empathy and sorrow over what I've done mutes and is replaced by forward planning.

James wants to look after me at this moment, and it is best that I let him. Everything from this moment on has to be carefully considered and planned out. There must be no doubt in his, or anyone's, mind that I am suffering. That I am grieving. That I had absolutely nothing to do with this.

I collapse lightly into his side, as though all the strength from my body had evaporated. And I suppose it has even though I've locked my guilt away. I know it's still there. Waiting for its chance to ruin my life.

I can't let it though.

What's done is done and losing everything I've worked so hard for won't change the outcome of tonight. May will still be dead whether or not I win the party seat.

James wraps his arm around me and pulls me into his chest, whispering calming nothings towards me. His chin is resting on the top of my head. He's so warm that I can't help but melt into his touch. If I married him we'd make such an attractive couple. So stable and respectable. I fight down the smile that's tugging at my lips as I imagine our wedding day and the coverage it would garner. Should we get married before or after I secure the top position in the country? Before I think. It seems less showy.

"They won't let me see her," I keep my words small and airy. Too often in life, I've learned that the way to a man's heart is to appear lesser than. Less passionate. Less loud. Less capable.

"It's probably for the best. There will be another time to say goodbye." He replies and squeezes my arm as though he's trying to put me back together. I'm not broken though. At least not in the way he thinks I am.

"You dropped this by the way." He places my phone to the side of me. Of course he'd been the person holding me back when I'd tried to run towards May. Nobody else would have cared enough to intervene in that moment. Nobody else would have known it was my sister diving towards her concrete grave.

"Can you take me home?" I ask him, knowing he won't be able to resist. Who in their right mind could leave someone alone after something so horrifying? He makes eye contact with a paramedic who gives him a brief nod.

"Of course." He replies, taking me by the hand and leading me from the back of the ambulance. I keep the foil blanket over my shoulders for the waiting photographers who have now descended.

One of them notices me and then they all shout over each other trying to get my attention.

I keep my features hollow and neutral, tears streaming down my face until finally I let the wind catch in the blanket and it gets whipped from my shoulders. I'm a broken woman and will be on the front page of all the papers tomorrow. Everyone will be united in their sympathy for me. Everyone will briefly be putty in my hands and I must be sure to mould their pity into something useful sooner rather than later.

My competition in the race for the party seat will no doubt advise, out of concern, that perhaps I should step down from this current election. That after what happened to my sister I would be better off living life slower until I'd processed everything. How am I going to argue against that though? Simple. I'll tell them all how much May supported me over the years, how proud she was of all my achievements and how much she'd hate herself if her death was the reason I gave up on my dreams. The press would eat it up.

If Andrew has done his job properly then this will all look like a suicide.

Which will be backed up by interviews with those who knew May. Who knew she'd chosen to work remotely because she couldn't take the company in the office.

The hotel receptionist who would confirm that she'd been staying near my office for far longer than May had owned up to.

The Inspector, James, would confirm that she'd been acting erratically and full of paranoia.

And finally her sister, who would confirm that it had been her big sister sending her threatening notes. That May had in fact lost what tenuous grip on reality she had left.

Her medical records would be investigated, the two stays in a mental institute would line up with all we had to say and my sister's reputation would be forever tarnished.

But mine though?

My reputation would be remembered as the politician who lost somebody to such a frightful disease. Who used her power to advocate for better mental health diagnoses and treatments. Who made it her mission in life to half the number of suicides in a decade.

Maybe I'll name an act after her, a way to keep her around when she doesn't exist anymore. Yes, that will play well with the public, and probably secure me a second term.

For now though I'm stuck in the here and now. With James by my side as we walk away from the scene of my sister's death, hand in hand, highlighted by a hundred flashlights as we start the next chapter of our journey together.

It's all more perfect than I could have ever imagined.

Chapter Thirty:

It's been six months since my sister's funeral.

Six months since I stood before a swollen congregation and gave a eulogy that still, to this day, is being quoted on social media.

More often than not they use a flattering photo of me taken on the day itself. Andrew made sure to capture my best angle, of course. I look elegant in my black dress, and my large sunglasses only serve to highlight the grief I felt that day. Because I did grieve for her. I'm still grieving for her.

May is the only person I think I'll ever truly love. And she lived as long as she did because of that love.

I know I'm a monster.

I know there's a side of me that acts too selfishly for acceptance. But when it came to her I was desperate to keep that side of me in check. I tried for so long to find any other option. A way to keep her in my life.

I'd meant what I'd said to Chris, all along I had been trying to protect her from danger. It just so happened that I was the danger she needed to be kept safe from.

The Sanctuary was supposed to have stopped her from ever remembering the night our parents died, or the argument I'd had with them over Samantha and the night Kayla had died. They'd moved heaven and earth to keep me out of juvie that week.

Favours were called in and palms were greased and eventually everyone in town accepted that it was a tragic accident, nothing more. Only me and Samantha knew the truth, but thanks to her reputation as a party girl, nobody listened and sooner or later she gave up. Or at least she had until she got the ridiculous notion of a tell-all book into her head. Of course we had to put a stop to that.

Somewhere, in the dark recesses of May's mind she'd known what I'd done to Kayla. But as a coping mechanism she chose to forget, and thanks to that first decision of hers, I've spent a lifetime keeping memories from her.

After our parents' funeral she'd confronted me at the wake. Accused me, openly, of planning their deaths. The guests had been shocked, hands had flown to their faces as they gasped. But due to her little candle incident at the funeral everybody dismissed it as hysteria. Perhaps if they hadn't things would never have gone so far.

Despite all my parents did for me in covering up my crime, they still let me down. The scandal they brought to our door with their money laundering could not be forgiven. I would have been tainted. I would never have become a politician people could trust. So I took care of business.

The first time May came out of the Sanctuary I could tell I'd lost a part of her, but so long as I still had her love then everything was okay I rationalised to myself. I let her believe she was always taking care of me, always looking out for me and that's the side of May I spoke about the day of her funeral.

My tears were genuine when I spoke of the magnitude of my loss. She had been the second most important thing in my world and now all I had left was my career.

Well, my career and James.

He all but moved into my house the day May died and we quickly married in a low-key ceremony attended only by Andrew and a few journalists we trusted. James is an orphan, too, and now we're both only children. It stops things from getting too complicated I suppose.

I still check my phone at 7 p.m. every night, expecting her to call me up and share tidbits about her day as we prepare dinner together. I don't think I'll ever stop expecting her to call. Grief doesn't care that I killed my sister. It wants to take hold of me anyway.

I miss her.

I miss her so badly that sometimes it takes my breath away.

The first time I noticed I was unable to take a deep breath, I rushed to the doctor, convinced I was somehow being punished for my sins.

It turns out it was nothing more than the amusingly titled air hunger which could be brought on by stress or anxiety. Both of these are now constant fixtures in my day since I ordered Andrew to push May from the roof.

Do I regret my decision?

Yes. Everyday.

No. Never.

It's hard to give a definitive answer to that question because my feelings are so conflicted. It feels like May's death was an inevitable conclusion I'd just been delaying for so many years. She was the one person in the world who knew all my secrets, and she was never truly aware.

Sooner or later her memories would have returned properly and I don't know how she would have reacted.

Would she have turned on me? Told the police of her suspicions? Burnt my life to the ground?

Or would she have spoken to me? Tried to understand. Loved me anyway.

I know which option I hope for, and which would have been true.

She would never have forgiven me for taking Chris away from her.

In fact she'd attacked me in my flat just after it happened because on some deeper level she could smell his blood on my hands. I'd been certain to clean every speck from her kitchen before we disposed of him, but still, I could tell that somewhere inside her mind she knew I'd robbed her of the man she'd loved.

There had been no other choice though. If he lived I would have lost her anyway.

And now, nearly six months to the day of her funeral I'm awaiting the results of the party election.

Given the scandal my opponent found himself embroiled in, there isn't a chance on earth that I won't win, which is why James has already popped out to get some champagne. Andrew will be on his way over with the official results shortly and the three of us will toast to my victory and lament over the person missing from the celebrations.

She's left such a big hole in my life that it needs mentioning at least twice daily. Sooner or later though people will forget, their sympathetic looks will fade and I'll have to find another angle with which to humanise myself.

I've suggested to Andrew that we set up a mental health charity in her name. One that provides care not only to the sufferers but to the people who love them as well. Because we need support too.

Andrew however had dismissed my suggestion as showboating.

I think Andrew needs to remember that I'm not above letting him go if I need to. He isn't the only sycophant in the world who wants to hitch their wagon to my success story. True, he has gotten less pushy since I let him take care of the May problem, but he still has ideas above his station.

On my wedding day, he had actually taken me aside and tried to tell me that I was making a mistake. James wasn't the one for me and that I couldn't trust him. I think Andrew would be happiest if he were the only person in my life I could turn to, but that's no way to live.

Yes. I need to keep an eye on Andrew. Make sure he hasn't outstayed his welcome.

The doorbell rings and with an excited cry, I move towards it, expecting to see Andrew standing there with an envelope in hand. Instead, peering through the peephole I see a large bouquet of flowers. I wonder if he arranged for these to arrive at the same time as he did. He's going to be so annoyed at the florist for arriving early.

I throw the door open and take the bouquet gratefully, making sure to thank the driver. My arms are full of white lilies and the pollen from them irritates my nose. These definitely aren't from Andrew. He knows these are my least favourite flowers. They're a harbinger of death in my eyes. I hadn't permitted a single lily at May's funeral such is my disdain for them.

With not much care I plonk the gift onto my kitchen counter. Still, I suppose it's nice of someone to send me a congratulatory gift. I shouldn't be so ungrateful.

Rooting through the cupboard I pull out a large glass vase and run the tap, filling it halfway. I place it down carefully on the side next to the sink and next reach into the drawer to locate my scissors.

In one slick movement, I release the stems from their cellophane wrapper and place them haphazardly into the vase - I'm not one for flower arranging so I'm sure James will redo it when he gets home.

Thinking of my husband I pull out three champagne flutes and silently pray that he's managed to find a pre-chilled bottle of bubbles for us to enjoy. It's not quite the same to toast a victory with room-temperature champagne.

A victory.

A long sought-after and hard fought for victory.

Today I am one step closer to the dream I've had since I was a child. Since the day I realised there was a way for me to be in charge.

Soon enough they will run the general election and I will spend every day between now and then proving my worth to the public. I need them to vote for me in their masses because I don't just want to win. I want to win by a landslide. That's the only thing that will make all the decisions I've made worth it.

That's the only thing that will make May's sacrifice worth it.

I pick up the cellophane and ball it up, but there's something hard in the middle. The gift note of course! I must make sure to send a note of thanks to the sender, I didn't want to appear ungrateful and it always pays to keep people happy.

I peel open the little white envelope and pull out the card.

I know what you did.

The world around me spins and I reach for my phone.

This is impossible.

This can't be happening again.

Epilogue:

Somewhere, on the other side of town, James places a crumpled florist's receipt into a nearby bin. His wife would have received the bouquet by now, and more importantly, she would have received the note he left.

People might question the sanity of a man who sleeps with the woman who killed the only family figure he ever had. They'd probably lock up the one who took it a step further and married her but James is quite sure of what he's doing. He's just keeping his enemy as close as can be. Until the time is right.

It's always better to topple your prey when they feel most invincible, and up until she received those flowers, he was quite sure that's how Isabella felt. She had just become the leader of her political party and she tied up all but one of her loose ends. He was certain that Andrew, the only person alive aware of her crimes, would have an untimely accident soon enough. A woman like Isabella doesn't like owing anyone favours for too long after all.

Agatha and her husband had been the only adults who'd shown any interest in James as he grew up, the only people who had shown him kindness. And for that they had earned the title of 'auntie' and 'uncle' in his heart. In truth there was no familial blood that ran between them, they were nothing more than an older couple who lived in the flat next door to his mother's.

But they meant more to him than either of the two people who had brought him into the world. They all but raised him into the man he was now.

His aunt had served Isabella for many years as her secretary. Agatha had spent more time in the office than she had at home, which suited his uncle fine. The two of them had an old-fashioned relationship, the kind where somehow two people seem to centre around each other despite never spending time together.

It had been odd to grow up alongside, but he was certain there had been true love between the two of them when his uncle died of a broken heart two months after his aunt took her fall in the office building. Isabella still wore the scarf that Agatha had knitted for her, and every time he saw it he wanted to pull it tight and wring her neck. But killing her was less than she deserved. She needed to suffer the most monumental fall from grace the world has ever witnessed.

It was when he was clearing out his Aunt and Uncle's house that he realised he had to make her pay. He was sitting on the floor of their bedroom overcome with grief at the unfairness of the world when he'd pulled a scrapbook from a drawer. A scrapbook full of press cuttings about Isabella. And within those pages of pride, he found an envelope with a hastily scribbled note inside.

Isabella can not be trusted.

His aunt's grasp on reality had started to wane as she aged, and her handwriting had followed suit, but he could still make out the words and they stung him to his core. What could this woman have possibly done to cause his aunt to leave this warning? His wonderful, kind, always thought the best of everyone, aunt. The woman had always been there for him, more so than his own parents. He had to know why Isabella thought she deserved to die.

At first, he'd called around to Isabella's office, wanting to confront her. But the receptionist hadn't let him up and now he was grateful for their interference. If she'd met him that day, full of questions and grief, then he wouldn't be in the position he is now. Ready to bring her world crashing down around her.

Losing May had been unfortunate. But if he'd intervened to save her life then all of his plotting so far would have been for nothing. And so he stood silently in the shadows as May walked through the doors onto the roof where he'd seen Andrew disappear moments before.

A part of him had wanted to call out and warn her, it really had. That's what he told himself each night. Besides, at least this way she didn't have to live through the chaos that the truth about her sister would bring to the world.

He did regret dismissing her worries about Andrew as well. She'd been so close to the truth but he wanted to be the one to reveal it. And so he let the inevitable happen. Isabella was the one who made the call though, the one who told Andrew to let her go, so at the end of the day his conscience about May's death was mostly clear.

He wondered, as he watched his wife sleeping next to him most nights, if that's what she'd said to Andrew the day they pushed his aunt down the stairs.

Let her go.

Three simple words to end a life. And he was adamant they had ended his aunt's. For a start, his aunt had never had a fall. She was steady as a rock, always had been. Would have been fantastic at American football had she had the inclination. When she planted there was no moving her.

You add that to the fact that his aunt's shoes were found unlaced and it was an open-and-shut case of murder as far as he was concerned. She always double-knotted her laces and had taught him to do the same. A fact his wife often made fun of him for. But nobody was interested in his theories, not when Isabella's tear-stained face was plastered on the front pages of the local press.

Funny how the CCTV had failed to capture the fall itself but had managed to grab the screenshot of Isabella, rising politician and local sweetheart, discovering her long-serving secretary's body. Once or twice he toyed with the idea of bringing Agatha's death up with her over dinner, under the guise of empathy of course, just to see what she'd say. He didn't trust himself enough though to play that game. It was too likely he would snap.

In the early days of their relationship, when he was investigating the notes being sent to Isabella, he wondered how she didn't recognise him. He knew for a fact his aunt kept a photo of him on his first day in uniform on her desk. She had been so proud of him, and had arrived an hour early to his graduation in her best hat, just to be sure she was in the front row. His own parents had slunk in halfway through the ceremony, already halfcut at midday.

But it was clear Isabella never recognised him. Clearly she wasn't as invested in his aunt as his aunt was in her. She'd erased all memory of Agatha from her consciousness, like the true sociopath she was. Thankfully she'd had a prior engagement the day of his aunt's funeral and the two of them hadn't crossed paths. He didn't like to think what would have happened if they had.

Speaking of the notes Isabella had been sent, he had May to thank for giving him an entry into his wife's life. He'd been the first to raise his hand for the case when it had come into the station. The married officers around him had mistaken his eagerness for lust and he was quite happy to go along with that story.

It made the whirlwind romance the two of them had undertaken even more believable. His colleagues were only too happy to speak about his keenness to help Isabella on that day, and every time they did it made his feelings for her more plausible to others.

Before he set eyes on her in person, he wasn't sure he had the stomach to truly go through with his plan. Too certain that the sight of her would make him sick, but it was quite the opposite.

There was something magnetic about her and despite telling himself it was all for show he did feel some attraction towards her. An attraction that had only continued to grow during their time together.

Maybe it was a power thing. When she lay beneath him at night, and he thrust in and out of her body until they were both spent, she had no idea that she was sitting in the palm of his hand. That one day he would destroy her and everything she worked for. Even now, walking in the cold November winds, the thought of it stirred him.

In a few more days he'd have all the evidence he needed.

Photos, statements, and forensic evidence to tie her to each and every case.

Kayla. Marcus. Samantha. Chris. May. Agatha.

He would make her pay for them all. The only one he'd yet to sort out was the case of her parents' accident, something he was working on.

One of the guys who'd worked on recovering the vehicle had apparently jotted down some discrepancies and was willing to talk for the right price. This vendetta had cost him an arm and a leg. Nobody wanted to talk against Isabella unless he made it worth their while. And he did so willingly.

Thankfully his wife was more than happy to pay for everything in their day-to-day life, a way to exert her power over him, so his money was his own and she asked no questions.

The idea of living without her though was becoming less and less appealing each day he spent by her side. He had grown used to her presence, despite the rage it sometimes caused in him. But he had to do what he had to do. There was no going back now.

He hoped that when the news broke Andrew would step forward and confess. That sycophant was a thorn in his side, always butting into their relationship, and once or twice he'd considered letting him go himself. But that would make him as bad as Isabella and his aunt wouldn't want that. Agatha always told him that he was better than that.

His aunt.

Agatha.

The women who'd loved him when all he'd known was anger and disinterest from the adults around him. He had to keep in mind who he was doing this for.

His phone rang, and he pulled it out of his pocket. Isabella's name flashed on the screen and he knew it would be to tell him about the flowers. She'd be going out of her mind now, wondering who had sent them and why. She knew her sister had been behind the original notes and he wondered if for a brief moment she worried May had come back from the dead to haunt her.

That could be a fun game to play over the next few days. To feed into his wife's guilt over her sister's murder. All he'd need to do is leave a few things lying around. He still had hold of her mother's locket, having retrieved it from May's body. That would be a good start.

Smiling to himself now James hits ignore on his phone, knowing she'd immediately redial him, and takes a turn down a street towards a supermarket. Lasagne for dinner ought to push his wife into a bit of a state. He knows it was her sister's favourite food; knows it was their mother's favourite recipe.

A friend he made long ago had managed to locate transcript copies of May's therapy sessions whilst she was institutionalised.

Institutionalised under her sister's insistence. He knows about the argument the night their parents died, and knows that May suspected her sister of doing something terrible, he just needs to work out what she did to their car to cause such a catastrophic accident. He knows so much and he's so close to making sure everybody else knows it all too. Isabella would regret the day she killed his aunt and all the days that followed. His phone rings again, as he knew it would and this time he answers, listening to her frantically worry down the line.

"Christ, okay calm down, I'll be home in five," he replies, picking up a chilled ready meal from the cabinet. "Don't worry, I'll bring dinner."

Acknowledgements

Where would an author be without the village that holds us up? Probably crying alone into a cup of coffee.

Where to begin? Well, with those who read the 'dump draft' of this book and helped encourage me to keep working on it - Viv, Charlotte, Terri, Liz & Ramona - thank you for being my most trusted pairs of eyes.

This time around I have a team of first readers that give me honest, much needed, feedback (good and bad) in no particular order thank you to: Hailey, Monica, Ashley, Faith, Robin, Deanna, Shari, Cheryl, Thesera & Shauntelle for all your support and encouragement.

And she'll kill me if I don't thank her, given how many voice notes and text messages she had to wade through. A massive thank you and shout out to my editor Allison - you're one of my biggest supporters and I'm so grateful the world joined our paths together.

Thank you to you, dear reader, for taking a chance on an indie author. You really do help dreams come true every time you do that.

 Finally, and I promise I'm nearly done here - thank you to my family, my husband and my kids for once again letting me disappear into my own imagination with very little complaining. One day I'll live in the real world I promise.

For updates and information on future releases please visit

www.smthomas.co.uk

And join the mailing list.

Or you can find me on Facebook (**smthomaswrites**), Instagram (**smthomas_author**) and occasionally TikTok (**sm_thomas0**).